Luther, Wyoming

LUTHER, WYOMING

TOMAS ALAMILLA
AND MARIO ACEVEDO

FIVE STAR
A part of Gale, a Cengage Company

Copyright © 2021 by Tomas Alamilla
Five Star Publishing, a part of Gale, a Cengage Company

ALL RIGHTS RESERVED.
This novel is a work of fiction. Names, characters, places, and incidents are either the product of the author's imagination, or, if real, used fictitiously.

No part of this work covered by the copyright herein may be reproduced or distributed in any form or by any means, except as permitted by U.S. copyright law, without the prior written permission of the copyright owner.

The publisher bears no responsibility for the quality of information provided through author or third-party Web sites and does not have any control over, nor assume any responsibility for, information contained in these sites. Providing these sites should not be construed as an endorsement or approval by the publisher of these organizations or of the positions they may take on various issues.

LIBRARY OF CONGRESS CATALOGING-IN-PUBLICATION DATA

Names: Alamilla, Tomas, author. | Acevedo, Mario, author.
Title: Luther, Wyoming / Tomas Alamilla, Mario Acevedo.
Description: First edition. | [Waterville] : Five Star, a part of Gale, a Cengage Company, 2021
Identifiers: LCCN 2020003455 | ISBN 9781432875299 (hardcover)
Subjects: GSAFD: Western fiction.
Classification: LCC PS3601.L3264 L84 2020 | DDC 813/.6—dc23
LC record available at https://lccn.loc.gov/2020003455

First Edition. First Printing: April 2021
Find us on Facebook—https://www.facebook.com/FiveStarCengage
Visit our website—http://www.gale.cengage.com/fivestar
Contact Five Star Publishing at FiveStar@cengage.com

Printed in Mexico
Print Number: 01   Print Year: 2021

Para mis familiares y los cuentos de vaqueros

Chapter One

April 1873

Adam Sanchez said, "Tess, please. We can find a way to make this work."

Tess Buchanan stood on the threshold of her father's house and propped the door open against one shoulder. "Adam, we've gone over this. I can't see you anymore." She regarded Adam with doe eyes, huge and beautiful, and he wondered how he could've misread them. Until two days ago, he was certain she was as much in love with him as he was with her.

He felt the moment backfire, and it left him reeling.

A breeze lifted the aroma of lilacs off the Virginia landscape. Adam was dressed in his best clothes, which meant his least-worn trousers, shirt, and coat, laundered or brushed clean. He worried the brim of his hat between his fingertips. Inside him, the stain of horror from the war—eleven years past—had just started to fade, and now he felt another stain color his heart.

A stain of rejection.

He wanted to ask, *why?* But he knew.

Tess was the only daughter of a federal judge. She had schooling. She was high society. At one time she had been a debutante.

What was Adam? A comanchero from the New Mexico Territories, a Mexican-Comanche half-breed. For the last fourteen-plus years he had lived among these people on the East Coast. Fought in their war. Learned their language. Read their books. Taught himself to sound schooled. Understood their ways, both the straight and the crooked. Learned to cloak himself in their customs. And somehow fooled himself into thinking that, because they had needed him and praised him for his service, he was their equal.

In fact, he wasn't. They didn't regard him much more highly than any of the colored soldiers. Tess's father, Judge Gideon Buchanan, often reminded him of that. The first time Adam and the judge met, Adam had made sure to dress in a borrowed suit, which he decorated with his medal from the Grand Army of the Republic. But the judge pointed to the medal and dismissed Adam in a boozy slur—"Why should I be impressed? You only did what was expected of you"—before stumbling in the direction of a fresh bottle.

That was also a fact, but Adam didn't mention that he knew plenty of white men of the judge's station who hadn't done their duty. Educated malingerers who waved the flag and boasted of their patriotism, yet shirked behind their privileges and moneyed connections.

Despite her father, Tess's affection had been genuine. Once. Perhaps it still was.

Adam shifted his weight. The porch creaked beneath him.

"Tess," he said, weakly, and groped for something more to say, for a magic phrase that would make all that separated them disappear and have her tumble into his arms like she used to.

She shook her head. "Don't, please. That time has passed." She gazed downward, and the silence between them grew hard and bitter.

Adam tried to swallow the lump in his throat. What a dolt he'd been to pretend he could build a future with a woman like her.

"Tess," Judge Buchanan called from inside the house. "The water's a-boiling. I'd like my coffee now."

She looked over her shoulder, and then at Adam. Her face

softened with resignation, like she was trapped with no way to escape her obligations. "I have to go." She braced one arm against the doorjamb and started to turn from him. "Take care of yourself."

They locked eyes one last time, and, when she yanked her gaze away, it was as if the motion ripped his heart.

The door closed.

Adam stared at it in disbelief. He felt small, childish, wasting his time longing for something he was never meant to have. He backed away, turned around, and stumbled down the porch steps. His horse waited in the shade of a cottonwood.

The one woman among the dozens he had wooed—the one he had fallen for, the one he would change for—was the one who had spurned him. The irony burned, and it would be a long time before that ache healed, if ever. How many times in his youth had he told himself this kind of foolish heartbreak wouldn't happen to him. And yet here he was.

He reached his horse. From one of the saddlebags he retrieved his gun belt and cinched it around his waist. He found his spurs and buckled them in place. Last, he untied the bay mare's reins and hoisted himself onto the saddle. He paused and gave the judge's house one final appraisal. A fleeting notion entertained him, that Tess would come running.

But that hope quickly died.

In the distance a train whistle blew, and its echoing wail nudged Adam to get moving. He snapped the reins and guided the horse west.

Chapter Two

Sheriff Nelson Cook looked at the money on his desk. A bundle of ten-dollar United States notes neatly bound in twine.

Cook remained still, leaning back in his chair, right leg stretched out, right hand perched on the edge of his desk, a mere twitch away from the Remington revolver on his lap. *A couple of saddle tramps walk in on a Saturday morning and toss a stack of cash like this on your desk, you better get your nerves sizzling and take in everything with your eyes peeled wide open.*

He stared at the man who had just dropped the greenbacks, then eased his gaze over to the man's companion beside him. The two looked alike. Tall, maybe six foot, though the fellow on the left was a bit taller. Identical gray eyes creased with crow's feet. Craggy faces that looked like the hard scrabble of the hills surrounding town. Trail dust coated the stubble on their cheeks and chins.

They dressed alike, too. Long, grimy coats swaddled their ropy physiques. Faded hats looked little better, with brims gone limp from too much time under the rain and sleet. Gray stains matted the bandanas cinched around their necks. They reeked of human sweat, horse sweat, horse piss, horse shit, and, most of all . . . trouble.

Their coats were open to show cap-and-ball revolvers in holsters hung from shabby leather belts festooned with misshapen cartridge pouches. But the men took special care to make easy moves and kept their hands in plain sight.

Just as well. Cook had managed to keep blood off his hands during the War Between the States. But that didn't mean his hands were clean. He had served as a sergeant in the Provost Guard of the Union Army, an assignment that had made him appreciate just how profitable desperation could be. Smugglers, deserters, gamblers, and prostitutes were all willing to pay stacks of cash for the law to look the other way. Copperheads were especially generous. Cook had made a tidy fortune working the crooked corners of the law. Too bad he lost that money on bad bets, both on and off the card table.

"Fifty bills," said the first man. "That's five hundred dollars."

"I can do the arithmetic." Cook dragged his hand across his trousers to rub sweat off his palm. "Before you tell me what this is about, how about telling me your names?"

"Charles West," the older one said. He nodded toward his companion. "That's Kevin West. We're brothers."

Cook brought his left hand up and rubbed his mustache. *Brothers . . . thought so.* The names didn't sound familiar. Maybe they were using aliases. "What brings you boys to sparrow-fart Wyoming?"

"Rumor has it, Luther's the kind of place where people tend to be a little forgetful."

"Might be more than a rumor." Cook sat straighter but kept his right hand parked close to his gun. The West brothers had the look of hunted men who were tired of running. "Let me guess. You two have a past you'd like to leave behind, if possible."

Charles dipped his head. "One might say such a thing."

With his left hand, Cook pointed to the money. "And that's to make sure I keep my mouth quiet about you being here."

Both brothers nodded.

Cook leaned back again. "The complication is, I have a

responsibility to keep order in this little corner of God's creation."

"We aim to live here peaceably."

"A noble enough concern. But, sincere as your words may be, trouble may follow you surely as night follows day."

Kevin shifted. His boots scraped the floor, and spurs jingled. Cook's pulse hitched. His hand flexed toward his revolver.

Charles stretched his arm across his brother's chest. "First hint of trouble—"

"You two jump on your horses and ride the hell out of town," Cook blurted. "I'm not going to let anyone get hurt or killed because of you."

Charles squared his shoulders. "Fair enough."

Cook gestured to Kevin. "I want to hear it from him."

The younger brother's mouth twitched and cracked the dust plastered around his lips. "Like my brother agreed to. Trouble comes to Luther, we beat hooves down the trail."

Cook allowed himself a tiny smile of triumph as he planned for a bigger score. No doubt the West brothers were criminals on the lam. If they could afford to bribe him with a year's salary, that meant they kept the lion's share of their loot hidden someplace. How much? A thousand? Five thousand? More? Money like that didn't often fall into a man's hat. Which meant a robbery. Maybe a shooting or two. Maybe a killing. Which meant a bounty. Probably a hefty one.

Luther had no telegraph, but Cook would be certain to check the gazettes and broadsheets on his desk to see if they made mention of outlaws who matched the Wests' description.

The sheriff put his left hand on the money and pulled it closer. This five hundred dollars was simply a deposit on future earnings. At the first notice of a reward, Charles and Kevin West would be riding toward the cemetery laid flat in pine boxes.

"Found a place to stay?"

"The saloon hotel," Kevin answered. Carefully, he slid his hand into one pocket of his coat, moving so slowly that skin could be heard scraping against rough cloth. Just as deliberately, Kevin withdrew his hand, holding a key attached to a brass fob. "Room number thirteen."

The bad omen plucked the sheriff's nerves. *Thirteen?*

But that was just a number. He had learned during the war that superstition and luck didn't run on parallel tracks. Plenty a righteous man had taken a random minié ball through the head.

It was good luck that had brought the West brothers and their dirty money to him.

And more luck would bring the bounty on their heads and make Sheriff Nelson Cook a wealthy man.

Chapter Three

Sheriff Cook settled into his office chair with a cup of coffee and tried to forget about the West brothers. But questions nagged him like burrs stuck to his ankles.

Nothing about the Wests seemed familiar. Cook thumbed through the stacks of newsprints at his elbow. He unfolded the most recent edition of the *Rawlins Gazette* and skimmed the articles. Maybe he had read about them earlier but dismissed the details. No doubt they were on the run. From what? A hold-up? Of a bank? A train? A payroll?

For sure they were hiding from the law. Yet they had come to him to keep part of their secret, so they feared something worse than a man with a badge. Who and why?

Cook felt his nerves tug in opposite directions.

One choice was to do what he'd agreed to. Keep his head down and act dumb. The choice he'd made earlier when he'd taken the Wests' bribe.

The other choice was to lean on the West brothers and pry loose the rest of their secret. But, if he learned it, he would become a party to their conspiracy as if they were handcuffed together. A lawman in collusion with a pair of malefactors like these two was destined for a stint in prison.

Cook's eyes followed the words on the gazette, but nothing stuck in his mind. His apprehension, already screwed tight, screwed even tighter with the impression of being watched.

He lowered the newspaper and looked toward the window

facing the street. The curtains were drawn, but, if anyone were peeking inside, their silhouettes against the fabric would give them away.

No one was there.

The front door was closed. The jail room to his left was empty, the back door locked.

Satisfied he was alone and sheepish that his anxiety had gotten the better of him, he exhaled in relief and rewarded himself with a swig of warm coffee. He turned back to the gazette.

A floorboard to his left squeaked. The coffee in his mouth turned sour.

Reaching for his pistol, Cook whipped about in his chair.

A pair of revolver muzzles gaped before his eyes, the bores big and dark as railroad tunnels. His hand froze an inch from his gun. His throat felt like he'd choked on freezing mud. He focused down the length of the shiny barrels to cylinders pregnant with lead bullets.

Cook was a trigger pull from death, and he raised his eyes to identify his assassin.

The face was round. Tanned to a rich brown hue like hand-dyed buffalo hide. Shiny, dark eyes twinkling with mischief. High cheekbones. Fleshy lips drawn into a broad smile.

Adam Sanchez. His brown canvas riding pants, blue-and-white striped shirt, and black hat all looked store-bought new.

Cook spit his coffee. It dribbled down his vest and spotted the lap of his trousers. "The hell you doing?"

Adam lowered the pistols. "Big hello to you, Sheriff Cook."

Cook felt his blood slowly warm and his nerves unwind. He wiped coffee from his mustache and chin and gazed past Adam to the jail room. "How the hell did you get in here?"

"One of my tricks. A skill much appreciated by married women when I sneak in and out of their boudoirs." Adam didn't hide his conceit.

If nothing else, Adam's chicanery seemed to have sharpened since Cook had teamed up with him after they'd both been mustered out of the army. Adam was an oddity who had snagged Cook's curiosity and friendship. Not many Mexican-Comanche half-breeds made it a point to migrate east and fight for the Union. Cook heard that Adam fought like it was a personal feud between him and Johnny Reb. After the war, Cook and Adam drifted from Pennsylvania and made a living selling things that didn't belong to them or riding alongside shady men who needed protecting. Their lives crisscrossed like rabbit trails until they finally broke ranks last year at Fort Leavenworth. Cook continued west, while Adam turned east in search of easy money and women of easy virtue.

Cook gestured for one of the pistols. Adam flipped the gun over and handed it to him, butt first. It was a Single Action Army Colt .45, blued shiny black like obsidian, with a short barrel, gold scrollwork, mother-of-pearl grips. A gilded medallion commemorating St. Louis, Missouri, decorated each side of the handles. "I thought you were partial to Colt Navys."

"A man's gotta change with the times."

Cook cocked the hammer and let it ease forward. "Which pimp did you take these guns from? Would I know him?" He returned the revolver to Adam.

"You might." Adam shoved both guns into their holsters. He wore two on a matching belt of black leather with silver conches and an ornate buckle. "But what difference would it make?"

"Where did you get that fancy Mexican gun belt?"

"Got it special made in El Paso del Norte."

"St. Louis. Mexico. What put the itch in your feet?"

Adam sat on the corner of the desk. "The world's got a lot to see."

"Doesn't explain why you've come to Luther. Couldn't be work 'cause you don't know the meaning of the word."

Adam lowered his gaze and his voice. "Needed to get some distance between me and a problem."

"That problem involve money or a woman?"

Adam slurred his answer. "A little of one, a lot of the other."

"Are you passing through or staying?"

"Not sure."

"You're welcome to stay with me. I got room at home. 'Course, I expect a grown man to earn his keep. I'm not feeding an extra mouth that's attached to a healthy set of arms and legs."

"I've got a little money to tide me over. And I'm not afraid of work." Adam's gaze roamed around the sheriff's office. To the Wyoming map on the wall. The rifle and shotgun resting in their stands, a Blakeslee cartridge box for the Spencer and bandoliers kept handy. A key ring hanging from a hook. A stuffed bull elk's head. A stack of bulletins and warrants tacked beneath. The aroma of burning cedar filled the room. A barrel stove wafting smoke warmed the coffee pot sitting on top.

"And you, *Sheriff* Cook." The confidence returned to Adam. "I'm not surprised to find you wearing a badge, though I did expect to see you perched where you could work the local angles. Seems the angles in Luther are mighty narrow."

"Things have changed since we last rode together."

Adam scanned the desk and wiggled his nose as if he could smell the stack of the West brothers' money in Cook's desk drawer. "Bet they haven't." He riffled through the newspapers and gazettes.

Cook slapped his hand on them. "What are you looking for?"

"What are you hiding?" Adam slid off the desk and walked to the coffee pot.

The question burned into Cook. He needed an excuse to get Adam out of the office and out of his hair without raising suspicion. Adam reached for one of the metal cups hung on the wall behind the stove, then for the coffee pot.

A gunshot rattled the window. Loud, from a rifle, not a pistol.

Cook jumped to his feet. Adam hastily set the pot back on the stove. Eyes narrowed and visibly worried, he looked over his shoulder at Cook.

Chapter Four

Jake Jason had just propped open the door to the Mountain View Saloon and Hotel when Charles and Kevin West entered. Not much happened in Luther, so the arrival of the two strangers made Jake wonder what had brought them into town. He hoped they'd be generous with their money.

The West brothers had appeared an hour after sun-up, trail dust sloughing from their clothes and boots, one of them with a set of saddlebags draped over his shoulder. They had been polite enough, not saying much other than introductions, paying a week's rent—three bucks—for a private room with two beds. They'd gone upstairs to the room, then a moment later clomped back down without the saddlebags and headed to Sheriff Cook's office across the street. That made Jake speculate even more about what these two men were up to.

A man comes into town as trail worn as these two were, the first items to attend to should be getting a meal and washing up. But they hadn't even removed their spurs. Whatever words they shared with Cook must have been mighty important. Jake knew the conversation had to be about money, money that carried a strong taint to it.

He stood behind the bar counter and mopped his eggs with a slice of toast. The creak of floorboards made him look toward the door. The West brothers had returned to the saloon.

Charles, the older and taller of the two, came straight to the bar. He grimaced and pulled at his collar as if tired of his own grime. "How much for a bath?"

"Fifteen cents."

"Where's the barbershop?" Charles's hair hung in greasy curls past his ears. Several days' worth of beard darkened his chin and jaw.

"Ain't one in town. Daryl Anderson at the general store offers haircuts and shaves, but only barely, if you ask me. But he don't open 'til ten."

Charles glanced at the clock above the bar mirror. Jake knew what it said: eight twelve.

"If you don't mind waiting for my girl Lucy," Jake said, "she'll draw your bath, and she does barbering, too. She'll do the both of you, fifty cents."

Charles's eyes narrowed, and he gave a dirty smirk.

Jake added, "Strictly barbering."

Charles flipped back his coat and reached into a trouser pocket, revealing a holstered revolver on his hip, which he carried like a much-appreciated tool rather than for mere decoration.

Jake was used to seeing guns—rifles, shotguns, pistols—as necessary in these parts as shovels and axes. But locals didn't go about wearing a gun belt like what Charles wore. He'd bet Kevin wore a similar holster. What brought these shootists into town, and why would they make it a point to see the sheriff? Usually men like them avoided the law.

Charles placed an assortment of coins on the counter.

Jake pushed his thoughts back on track. Counting two quarters and three nickels, he slid them into his hand. "It'll be a half hour. Lucy's gotta put water on the stove."

Kevin pulled a chair from a corner table and sat with his back to the wall, facing the bar. "Ask him about breakfast."

"Eggs," Jake replied. "Johnny cakes. Fresh bacon and chops. Oatmeal. Apple crisp. Coffee."

"Tell 'em eggs and bacon," Kevin said. "Buttered toast if he's got any and a helping of the crisp."

"For sure. Twenty cents for two plates. The coffee's on the house."

"We'll start with coffee." Charles laid another quarter on the bar. "Keep the change."

Jake took the coin and his breakfast plate and walked to a door at the end of the saloon. He entered a kitchen already stuffy from a fire inside the stove and dropped the plate into a washtub.

Lucy was at a table, already hard at work shucking peas into a bowl. Her real name was Chinese, Lui Gaowa. Like most everyone else in these parts, she'd drifted into town like a wind-blown seed and planted roots. Jake told her to put a bucket of water on the stove for the Wests' baths and passed along their breakfast order, then asked her to fetch her barbering kit after fixing breakfast. After pulling two ceramic mugs from the pantry, he filled them with hot coffee from a blackened pot on the stove.

Cups in hand, Jake returned to the saloon. Charles had taken a seat next to Kevin, his back to the adjacent wall where he faced the kitchen door. Jake placed the cups on their table and returned to his place behind the bar.

A voice in his head nagged him, cautioning that the West brothers were nothing but trouble. He was reaching for a broom when he caught a shadow in the entranceway.

The next moment, a huge man loomed outside the open saloon door. The man was bear big. Grizzly-bear big. A dense beard, bushy eyebrows, and thick, tangled clumps of hair spilling from under his floppy hat added to the ursine appearance.

The man's eyes smoldered with menace, and the Winchester rifle in his hands told Jake the stranger had murder in mind. Dirt and grime stained his clothing—a green vest over a pale-blue shirt, buff-colored canvas trousers, boots scarred from abuse. A revolver was tucked inside a leather waist belt.

Jake kept still, letting only his eyes swivel to the West brothers. They sat with their heads down, sipping coffee, deep in hushed conversation.

Jake locked gazes with the big man. He'd noticed Jake's glance to the right. The stranger's already cruel expression got a little more cruel and projected a warning. *You move, you say anything, you die.*

Jake's heart galloped. He could see Sheriff Cook's office behind the stranger, a hundred feet away across the street. But, unless Cook somehow intervened in the next minute, that hundred feet might as well be a hundred miles.

A coach gun remained out of reach under the bar. Jake had yet to fire it in anger. He had yet to shoot at anyone—he was no killer—and he clenched his fists to keep his fingers from quivering.

The big man gripped his rifle in both hands and entered the bar, quietly, surprising considering his bulk. He pivoted toward the West brothers, brought the Winchester to his shoulder, and sighted down its barrel.

Jake watched, helpless, his throat closing, his tongue turning into a piece of dry leather.

A floorboard creaked.

Kevin raised his head. His eyes popped wide, the whites shining like peeled eggs. He managed to whisper, "Jesse," when the man fired.

The rifle blast boxed Jake's ears. Smoke billowed from the muzzle.

Kevin toppled to one side.

Fast as a rattlesnake, the man levered the Winchester. An empty cartridge whirled from the chamber and pinged on the wooden floor.

Charles bolted upright, reaching for his revolver.

Jesse fired again. Another cloud of smoke blossomed in the air. The second bullet slammed into Charles's breast. He tumbled over his chair and fell to the floor.

Jesse levered a fresh round and swung the rifle toward Jake, growling, "Don't make me kill you."

Jake trembled like a rabbit cornered along a fence. His ears rang from the echo of the rifle blasts. The odor of burnt gunpowder stung his nose. He stepped backwards until he bumped against the shelves and rattled the rows of bottles.

The kitchen door cracked open. Lucy poked her head and one arm around the edge, a butcher knife in hand.

Staring at Jesse, hands open and raised, Jake found himself yelling, "Don't shoot! Lucy, get back in the kitchen." Out of the corner of his eye, he saw her disappear.

Jesse plowed through the gun smoke fouling the saloon. He kicked the chairs aside and crouched between the West brothers. Blood pooled on the planked floor.

Charles lay on his back, gurgling and spitting up blood. His legs jerked, thumping his spurs against the wooden floor.

Jesse reached behind his back and produced a hunting knife. He planted a knee on Charles's torso, put weight against it, and traced the blade across the dying man's naked throat.

Jake imagined the cold steel slicing through his neck. He winced, closed his eyes, and felt his legs weaken. He heard Charles kick once, then heard nothing else except for Jesse's clothes rustling and the floorboards creaking beneath him.

Jake swallowed the lump of terror and opened his eyes.

Jesse was wiping the bloody knife on Charles's lapel. He returned the knife to its sheath, then tapped the pockets of Charles's coat. He did the same to Kevin next, sliding his hand into the younger man's coat pocket and withdrawing the room key on its brass fob.

Jesse held up the key and said something, but the words were lost on Jake, who stood frozen in horror. Shaking the key again, Jesse raised his voice. "This one of yours?"

Jake nodded. He pointed upstairs.

"Anyone else here?"

Jake gulped and forced himself to answer. "J-just me and Lucy."

Jesse shoved the key and fob into a vest pocket. Winchester at the ready, he stood and lumbered toward the stairs. He climbed them quickly, leaving bloody boot prints behind him.

Chapter Five

The blast had come from across the street.

Cook hoped it was the careless handling of a rifle, or an idiot shooting a coyote or a stray dog within the town limits. He hoped for anything except the worst . . . and the most obvious.

The West brothers is what burned through his mind.

A second shot confirmed his fears. Revolver in hand, he parted the window curtain and studied the shadow beneath the awning across the front of the Mountain View. The entrance was open. All quiet. Three horses were tied to a hitching rail along the wooden sidewalk. Two belonged to the West brothers, no doubt. And the third? His gaze swept the street. The feed store to the right was still, as was the blacksmith's shop next door. The general store to the left was shuttered and dark. No horses in sight. No people in sight. The street was as quiet as a tomb.

His thoughts lashed back to the Wests' money. He'd made a simple contract with the brothers. Take their cash and keep quiet. But whatever trouble they'd tried to run away from had curled back to bite them. And maybe him as well.

Cook holstered his revolver and put on his derby. He crossed the room and snatched the Spencer repeater. He kept the carbine's magazine loaded, and he cocked the hammer, then levered the first round into the chamber.

"What do you think?" Adam kept his eyes trained on the window tense as a dog ready to attack or run.

"Don't know." Cook approached the door, the Spencer at the ready. "I need you to keep me covered."

Adam drew one revolver. "Like old times, no?"

"Unfortunately. And I'd hoped those escapades were behind us." Cook opened the door, prepared to duck back. He stared at the saloon, then down the street in both directions. Still empty.

Hesitantly, he crossed the silent and desolate dirt expanse. It was only forty paces across but felt like a mile. With every step, the bull's eye he imagined on his chest grew bigger and bigger. Adam stepped lightly behind him, Colt raised, gaze swinging from window to window to door and back up toward another window.

Cook halted by the saloon entrance and nodded at Adam to get ready. He crouched, raised his pistol, and clicked back the hammer. Then, hugging the doorframe, he glanced inside. Gun smoke stung his nostrils.

Jake Jason stood behind the bar counter, back against the shelves, upraised hands shaking, looking like all the blood had been wrung from his face. He stared down at something off to his left.

Carbine level, finger on the trigger, Cook stepped in.

The West brothers lay on the floor, their bodies in a pool of blood the size of a mattress. Charles's neck was slit open, like a hog waiting to get skinned and quartered. Whoever had slaughtered the two brothers was a man too comfortable with killing.

The weight of the savagery pressed upon Cook. He'd seen plenty of bloodshed during the war, and this carnage reminded him that humans never seemed to weary of acting like monsters.

A trail of bloody boot prints led across the room to the stairs. Cook's gaze sought Jake's. "Who did this?"

Jake's voice shook. "A big fellow. With a big Winchester."

"One man?"

Jake nodded like his neck was on a spring. "They called him Jesse. He's in room thirteen."

Cook realized his plans for a quick fortune had collapsed and threatened to bury him in the rubble of murder. *You play the odds with bad money, don't be surprised when it comes back to haunt you.*

He panned the ceiling with the Spencer, ears pricked to home in on Jesse. With Adam's help they should be able to corner him. Cook glanced back toward his old buddy and saw with a jolt that Adam was gone. It wasn't like him to turn tail. *Where did he go? Goddamn him.*

The scuffling of boots on the floor above caught his attention. As sheriff, it was his job to keep the peace no matter the risk. He looked at Jake. "You got a gun?"

The barkeep reached under the counter and withdrew a short, double-barreled shotgun. Cook thought of asking that he follow him, but Jake's quivering hand said the barkeep was just as likely to shoot him in the back. Instead, Cook said, "Stay here. Any troublemaker comes in, let him have it."

Jake gulped and aimed the gun, trembling, toward the saloon door.

Cook approached the bottom of the stairway. He tipped his derby back and craned his neck to take in as much as he could. Drunks, scalawags, and gambling cheats he could deal with. But this job didn't pay enough for him to confront a cold-blooded killer on his own.

Slowly, he climbed the steps, planting his feet along the left edge, close to the wall, where the boards were less likely to creak. Step by step, he ascended, his heart climbing higher into his throat with every footfall.

Two-thirds of the way up, he halted to stand tiptoe and get a worm's eye view of the landing. Two halls intersected at a right angle with him at the corner. The door at the far end was open, the last of six rooms facing the street. A quick scan at the order of the brass numbers on the doors confirmed that last door had to be room thirteen.

Bad luck thirteen.

Cook wiped his sweaty palms across the Spencer's wooden stock. Well, if there was to be bad luck, then dear God in heaven, heap it on that stranger Jesse.

Cook's mouth felt dry as summer dust. Heart banging in his chest, he climbed the remaining steps and onto the landing. A shadow wavered across the doorway of the room. It had to be Jesse, moving about and blocking the sunlight outside.

Cook eased toward the door. The hair stood up on his arms and the back of his neck. Index finger taking the slack out of the trigger, he leaned into the open doorway.

Jesse stood between the door and a bed, the Winchester held loosely in one hand, his other bear paw–sized mitt digging into open saddlebags on the mattress. Cook glimpsed money stacked inside. Bills in tens, twenties, bundled together.

Distracted by the sight of so much money, Cook let his Spencer drift off mark. Belatedly, he caught movement in the corner of his eye as Jesse whirled and brought up his rifle. Cook swung the carbine back into position but realized he'd missed his chance.

The men stood eight feet apart, trading glares, rifles aimed at each other's chests.

"You squeeze that trigger, sheriff," Jesse growled, "and you're a dead man."

Cook answered, "This gun of mine is gonna do more than tickle your liver."

"Don't matter," Jesse replied. "I ain't afraid to die. Are you?"

Chapter Six

Sheriff Cook and Jesse glowered at one another, each man one twitch from getting his ribcage blasted open.

Jesse's eyes burned with a frightening resolve, like no amount of bullets could stop him. "Just lower your gun and walk away." The words rumbled from deep in his throat. "What's in the saddlebag is no business of yours. You let me keep this money, I let you keep living."

But the standoff wasn't about money. It was about the badge Cook had pinned to his shirt and the kind of spine he claimed to have. If he backed down, then he might as well turn in the badge and sell his guns, shave off his mustache, and clean spittoons for a living.

He could turn away, give Jesse the impression he'd won. Then ambush the son of a bitch later. But the evil glint in Jesse's eyes told Cook the gunman would strike first.

Sweat beaded on Cook's brow and temples. It dripped down his cheeks, tickling like centipedes crawling along his skin. His hands grew clammy and slick. A breeze billowed the curtains at the open window behind Jesse, but the gust of air offered no relief.

Adam Sanchez appeared in the window, moving slow and snake-like, balanced on the wooden awning that shaded the front sidewalk. Hat set low and leading with one revolver, he slipped through the window and into the room, rising like a cobra behind Jesse, both pistols drawn, hammers silently cocked back.

Relief surged deep inside Cook, but he bottled it up and fought to keep his eyes locked on Jesse. Minutes ago he had cursed Adam for deserting him, when his friend had actually roped the odds back in his favor.

"Listen, Jesse." Cook forced himself to speak calmly and not spook his adversary. "Take your finger off the trigger."

Jesse's face tightened. "Why the hell should I do that?"

"Because someone is behind you with a pair of loaded .45s. I'm giving you the chance to walk out of this room with your kidneys whole and in place."

Jesse tilted his head a bit. No fear in his face, only anger and disbelief.

"Easy now," Adam said in a soft lilt.

Jesse's expression remained hard. The man had ice water in his veins.

"Take your hand away from the trigger," Cook ordered.

Jesse's nostrils flared like a bull's. His face reddened like freshly cut meat. He released his right hand and held the rifle by the forestock.

"Now drop it on the bed."

Jesse tossed the Winchester sideways. It bounced on the mattress.

Adam flicked Jesse's hat off with one revolver and poked him with the other. "Hands on your head."

Jesse rested his huge mitts on his hairy scalp. His eyes never left Cook or warmed one degree.

Cook advanced two steps and jammed the barrel of his Spencer into Jesse's gut. He plucked the Webley RIC revolver from the big man's belt and dropped it on the bed, then stepped back and to the side. "Now kiss the rug."

Jesse glanced at the floor, brought his gaze back to Cook, and spat. The gob missed the sheriff. The tail of the spittle clung to Jesse's beard.

Adam cocked his leg and popped his boot against the back of Jesse's right knee. The big man's leg buckled, and his hands snatched downward to keep himself from falling.

Cook motioned with the rifle. "Keep going."

Jesse lowered himself to the floor. "You don't know who you're messing with, Sheriff."

"Enlighten me." Cook rested the muzzle of his rifle against Jesse's temple. "What's your beef with the West brothers? You working for someone?"

Jesse's face closed like a gate had swung shut in his mind. He pressed his nose against the carpet and clenched his jaw.

Adam holstered his revolvers and kicked Jesse's legs apart. He pulled a blood-stained hunting knife from a sheath on the back of the man's belt and tossed it to the floor. Crouching between Jesse's boots, he searched them, then gave the rest of him a pat down, but discovered only loose coins, rolling papers, lucifers, and a bag of tobacco in one vest pocket.

Cook approached the bed, where he tugged a rawhide lace from the nearest saddlebag and tossed it to Adam. "Bind his hands."

Adam grunted orders to Jesse, who joined his hands behind his back. In a couple of minutes Jesse's wrists were cinched, his fingers turning red. Adam held a revolver on him while Cook searched the room for anything the Wests might have brought besides the saddlebags. He checked under the beds and inside the armoire and dresser. All he found were folded sheets, an extra blanket—stuff that belonged here.

Cook picked up the Webley, gave it a quick study, and shoved it into his belt. He stuffed the loose cash back into the saddlebags, made sure none of the bills showed, and hefted both bags onto a shoulder. "You grab the Winchester," he told

Adam, "and the knife." He rapped the Spencer's muzzle against the back of Jesse's head. "On your feet."

Jesse struggled to get up. As he heaved to his knees, his face smoldered as red as his hands. He planted one boot on the floor and unfolded upright. God, the man was huge and imposing even tied up.

Adam slapped Jesse's hat back on his head. Cook prodded him in the back. "All right, downstairs."

They clomped into the hall and down the steps to the saloon floor. Adam brought up the rear. Jake Jason waited in front of the bar counter, the coach gun cradled in his arms. He'd quit trembling but remained pale-faced with sweat stains circling his neck and armpits. As soon as he saw Cook herding Jesse at gunpoint, his face regained its normal color, and the set of his shoulders relaxed. His house lady, Lucy, stood near the dead West brothers and waved a bar towel to shoo flies from the corpses.

Not surprising to Cook, they had an audience by now. Four men stood near the saloon door: the proprietor, Gunter Wald; Daryl Anderson from the general store; Burt Rex, the blacksmith; and Edward Blair, the undertaker. A couple of local women peeked in from outside. Everyone stared with apprehension at Jesse, like he was a dangerous, exotic beast on parade.

Anderson leaned on a table, a pencil in his hand, ready to start scribbling on a pad of paper. Besides being the town merchant and barber, Anderson fashioned himself the local newspaperman. "Sheriff, what do you know about this crime?"

"Not much, except what you see here." Actually, quite a bit more, but Cook had his secrets to keep.

The undertaker approached, a stocky man with an elfish face and eyes that hunted opportunities where others chose not to see. "It's best we bury these men as soon as possible. Before they get"—Blair's fingers fluttered as if searching for the right word—"gamey."

"Very well."

"It will cost money. Fifty cents apiece."

Cook hitched the saddlebags higher on his shoulder adjusting their weight. "I'll see what's available from the county treasury."

He gave Jesse another poke to urge him along. When they approached the saloon door, the two women outside skittered away like wary hens. About a dozen townsfolk waited in the street to witness his emergence with the murderous stranger. Adam kept his distance, watching Jesse and the crowd. A raven landed on a hitching post and studied the scene with beady, hungry eyes. Cook hoped the black bird's arrival wasn't an omen.

He stared at Jesse's back and wondered how to lasso today's events to his advantage. For one, there had to be a reward for a killer like Jesse. A man couldn't be that cold-blooded without experience. What about the money in the saddlebags? Cook could take a cut, throw some Adam's way, turn the rest in. If the bank or whoever claimed the amount was short, how was Cook to know what had caused the difference? Maybe the West brothers were wanted dead or alive, and, since they were dead, why not get a reward for them as well? Today's take might have been worth the anxiety of facing Jesse's Winchester.

Cook pushed Jesse into his office, dropped the Webley and the saddlebags on his desk, and plucked the key ring off the wall. "Adam, you wait here and watch the money." He shoved his prisoner into the only barred cell in the back room.

Jesse turned and scowled at him. "This could be your last chance, Sheriff. Let me go and hand over the saddlebags, and things will go easy for you."

Cook's pulse throbbed. He marched into the jail cell and smacked the butt of the carbine against Jesse's forehead. The big man gasped and stumbled against the wall.

"Threaten me again and you won't live to hang for what you did in the saloon." Cook kicked Jesse's feet from underneath him, and he tumbled to the floor. Crimson wrath overwhelmed Cook, and he lost himself in a storm of kicks and oaths. Finally, the rage ebbed and he panted, fatigued. Jesse lay on the floor, eyes closed, chest rising and falling with his shallow breaths. Blood seeped from his nose, a busted lip, and torn skin on his forehead. His hat lay in a crumpled wad beside him.

Cook inhaled once, held it for a moment, and let the breath out. He felt suddenly overwhelmed with guilt, not for giving this animal the thrashing he deserved, but for losing control. He adjusted his hat and glanced at the door to the office. Why hadn't Adam poked his head in to see what was going on? Cook gripped the knife sheathed at his hip and ordered Jesse to roll over.

The big outlaw grimaced and snorted. He cocked a leg and rolled onto his belly. Cook knelt beside him, laid the muzzle of the Spencer against one kidney, and cut the rawhide lace binding Jesse's wrists with a quick jerk of the blade. The lace unraveled, and Jesse clenched and unclenched his thick hands.

Cook backed out of the jail cell, locked the door, and returned to his office to put away the key ring and carbine. He had wanted to thank Adam for his quick thinking and daring but now meant to chastise him for not checking on the noise.

He found Adam slouched in the desk chair, his hat tilted back, the desk drawer open, a stack of the Wests' bribe money in one hand. "Tell me, Sheriff Nelson Cook, old friend, what is so peculiar about this cash?"

Chapter Seven

Adam Sanchez matched stares with Sheriff Cook and raked a thumb across the stack of money in his hand.

Cook's complexion turned purple like he'd swallowed poison.

Adam pointed to the saddlebags Cook had dropped on the desk earlier and shifted his finger toward another stack of money he'd taken out.

Cook lunged at Adam, grabbed a handful of shirt, and slapped the money out of his hand. He brought his face close to Adam's and hissed, "Shhh."

Adam tensed but kept his anger at bay. He glanced toward the back room, then at the money, and back at the sheriff. He'd gotten the message. Jesse couldn't know about the money Cook had stashed in the desk.

Cook hustled Adam to the front door and peeked outside. He ushered Adam over the threshold, followed him out onto the wooden sidewalk, and closed the door. The street was deserted save for a wagon raising dust in the distance. Lucy shuffled out of the saloon, a bucket weighing one arm. Blood stained her apron. She tipped the bucket and splashed pink water into the street. Without looking up, she turned around and disappeared back inside the saloon.

Adam smoothed his shirt.

Cook said, "Before you open your big yap, let me—"

"I know exactly what this is about. The paper band on the money in the saddlebags matches the band of that stack of tens

I found in your desk. First Bank of Kansas."

"Why the hell were you looking—"

"I was looking for a pen and ink to inventory the money." Adam backed away a step. "Didn't figure you were already knee deep in a scam."

Cook chewed his mustache. He leaned against the doorframe and gave his head a slow, guilty shake. "The West brothers came this morning. Offered a deal. I take their money and pretend I don't know anything while I let them stay in town."

"Where did they get the money?"

Cook replied with an embarrassed chuckle. "I got paid for not knowing. Remember?"

"And Jesse?"

"His presence certainly muddied the waters."

"Pretty brutal what he did to the West brothers. Like he enjoys murdering."

"Something tells me he does the killing for someone else, not that he minds the work." Cook brought his eyes back to Adam. They were sharp and piercing. "If you let on about the money you found—"

"The bribe money," Adam emphasized, grinning.

Cook drew his lips back and sucked through his teeth. "If Jesse knows too much about what he's not supposed to, he could say the wrong thing to a judge come his trial. That would further complicate my arrangement with the late West brothers."

Adam rocked on his heels. "How long have we known each other?"

"Fourteen years."

"Which only increases the depth of my disappointment in you."

Cook beetled his eyebrows. "In what way?"

"All that money and you never tossed me a cut."

"Now you disappoint me. You'll get a cut. If you hadn't been along, Jesse might have opened me up like a fish."

Cook reached for the door handle, but Adam put his hand on the door. "What's the problem?" Cook asked.

"My cut."

"First let's see how much we've got." Cook tipped his head toward the door. "If you don't mind."

Adam pulled his hand back and let Cook enter his office. Adam followed and shut the door.

Cook counted the stacks from the saddlebags while Adam tallied the amounts on a ruled tablet. Eleven stacks of five-dollar bills. Five thousand, five hundred dollars. Seventeen stacks of tens. Seventeen thousand dollars. Six stacks of twenties. Twelve thousand dollars.

"Thirty-four thousand, five hundred." Cook read the total, speaking low so Jesse couldn't overhear from the back-room jail cell.

"What about this?" Adam hefted the stack of tens he'd found in Cook's desk. "This makes it thirty-five thousand."

"Keep it," Cook replied. "Serves me right for leaving that lying around where any damn fool could've found it. And one did." He gave Adam a look and then strode across the room to a safe by the bookcase, crouched in front, and rotated the dial. He cranked the lever and opened the safe, revealing a box of cigars and a bundle of papers and envelopes. "Give me the money."

Adam tossed him the stacks, which Cook arranged like bricks. He shut the door of the safe, yanked the handle to make sure it was locked, and spun the dial. Returning to the desk, he snatched the sheet with the tally and walked to the barrel stove. He folded the sheet lengthwise, opened the stove, and fed the paper to the coals. It flared for a moment, and smoke puffed out the front of the stove to foul the room. Cook stared at the flame as if it were an oracle telling him something he wouldn't understand until it was too late.

He sighed heavily and told Adam it was time to question Jesse.

The big man was stretched on the jail cell bunk, arms folded, legs crossed at the ankles, his hat crammed beneath his big, hairy head. His eyes were clenched shut like he was pretending to sleep.

Cook rattled the cell door. "Wake up, you ugly bastard."

Jesse clenched his eyes shut tighter.

Cook grabbed a broom, stuck it through the bars, and jabbed the bristles against Jesse's face. Jesse jerked upright, snarling and cursing under his breath.

Cook set the broom aside. "You and I got some talking to do."

Jesse picked straw bristles from his beard and stood. Bruises and welts from the earlier beating mottled his face. "Go to hell."

"I've been there and back. Can't say I care for the place." Cook shook his ring of keys. "How long do you think you're going to stay in there?"

Jesse went *humph.*

"Days? Weeks? I could forget to feed you. Forget to give you water and soap. Things could get mighty ripe and miserable."

"Sheriff, do anything stupid like that and trust me, you'll come to regret it."

Cook looked at Adam and shook his head. "There he goes again with the threats." Cook leaned against the cell door and cocked an eyebrow. "Jesse, let's start over. How about you cooperate a mite and in return I treat you like a civilized human being. Maybe begin with breakfast?"

Jesse's eyes crinkled. He straightened his shoulders. "All right. Deal."

Cook set his key in the lock. He cleared his throat and winked at Adam, alerting him to be ready. "Come on out to wash up."

Jesse started for the cell door. The instant Cook clicked it open, Jesse launched himself at the sheriff.

Cook pulled the door back, then slammed it against Jesse's face. The outlaw's head rebounded, but he kept his grip on the door and bulled against it.

Adam drew a pistol and clubbed the barrel against the big man's skull.

Jesse stumbled, dazed. Blood stained his forehead. Cook grasped the door and banged it against Jesse's head, trapping his skull between the door and the frame. Jesse trembled from the blow, and he sank to the floor, his head still pinned.

Cook banged the door again. He scowled with gritted teeth, tendons corded at his throat. Adam had seen this expression before when men tore at one another like rats fighting to save themselves. What demon had Jesse unleashed inside his friend Cook?

Cook drew his Remington and cocked it. "Listen to me, you stupid son of a bitch." His breath came out ragged and labored. "Nothing says you have to live to see your trial. You could get shot trying to escape. Maybe make it to a horse only to get dragged to death. Fall into a ditch with your hands tied and drown. You decide. Now what's your full name?"

Jesse remained still.

Adam studied the big man. "Maybe you killed him."

Cook retreated a step. "If so, I did us all a favor. Push him back inside."

Adam dropped to his knees and set his hands on Jesse's head. The man's hair was warm and clammy with trail grime, perspiration, and blood. Adam heaved, budging Jesse's torso only enough to angle his head and neck to shut the cell door.

Cook turned the key in the lock, then removed it. He holstered his pistol. "Watch him."

Adam wiped his hands on a rag. Cook unlocked the backroom door and disappeared through it into the dazzle of bright sunlight. Adam heard a splash, like in a horse trough, and a few seconds later Cook returned with a bucket dripping water.

He doused Jesse with the bucket. Adam danced backwards to keep the water off his boots and pants. Jesse didn't move, and, for a moment, Adam thought the big man was dead.

Then Jesse shuddered, slowly straightened his arms, and pushed his chest off the floor. Water dripped from his face. He rocked onto his haunches and slid to the far wall of his cell. Blood trickled into his beard. "You win," he gasped and rested his head against the bricks. He whispered, "Jesse Norman."

Adam and Cook turned to him. Cook asked, "What?"

"I said, Jesse Norman."

The name Norman was familiar. A family of bank and payroll robbers from Missouri.

Cook continued the questioning. "What brings you this far west?"

"Ain't it obvious? The scenery."

"Where's the rest of your gang?"

Jesse smirked. "Two of 'em are lying in the saloon."

"How about the other Normans?"

This time, Jesse chuckled. "Reckon you're gonna find out real soon."

The demonic look from earlier flashed through Cook's eyes, and Adam feared the sheriff would fling open the cell door and stomp Jesse to death. In the years that Adam and Cook had ridden together, Adam had never seen Cook lose his cool like this.

Cook caught Adam staring. The sheriff hooded his eyes, and his face sagged in guilt. He beckoned Adam to follow him to the front office and was reaching toward a desk drawer when Adam asked, "What the hell has you so spooked about Jesse?"

Cook rubbed his forehead like a fever tormented him. "For the first time in my life I hear a clock ticking, and, when its alarm goes off, that will be the end of me."

"That's a load of horse shit." Adam unbuttoned his cuff, rolled his sleeve back, and showed off a jagged bullet scar that ran from wrist to elbow. "Remember when this happened? And you carry a worse one on your chest."

"That's a memory I'm trying to forget."

"And you said if we survived that ambush, life was downhill."

"So I did."

Adam unrolled his sleeve and buttoned the cuff. "Let go of that superstitious nonsense. From where I stand, if there's an alarm ticking, it's for Jesse, and it signals his appointment with the hangman."

Cook reached into the drawer and removed a small cardboard box. "If the Normans cause trouble, I'm going to need an assistant with some balls." From inside he drew a star-shaped metal badge embossed with *Deputy Sheriff.*

"By the authority vested in me as sheriff and chief constable of the town of Luther, in Carbon County, Territory of Wyoming, I hereby appoint you deputy sheriff, encumbered with all the rights and responsibilities thereof. Now raise your right hand."

Adam held still. The smart thing was to refuse the job, take his five hundred dollars, and make tracks. But, in the past, whenever trouble had clouded their future, he would ride tighter with Cook, his friend and often partner in crime. He wondered what Tess would've made of that. Would she have loved him more, or even less? *Probably less.*

Cook squinted. "There a problem?"

To blazes with Tess Buchanan, and all the rest back East. "Yeah, how much do I get paid?"

"I just gave you five hundred bucks."

"That was money to keep me quiet. How much am I gonna get *paid*?"

"Two bucks a week."

"I know a girl in St. Louis who makes two-fifty a throw."

"Put on a petticoat, bend over, and we'll see what you're worth."

"How about I raise my hand instead?"

"Now say 'I accept.'"

"I accept."

Cook handed him the badge. Adam pinned it to his left breast pocket.

Cook clapped Adam on both shoulders. "Don't lose the badge. It's the only one I got."

"Thought you'd be more worried about me."

"Freeloaders, I can always find. A new badge I have to special order."

Adam burnished the star with his shirt cuff. "Imagine me, a lawman."

"What's funnier is you making an honest living."

He winced at the truth of that, then shook it off. "What's next?"

"We wait for the stage to Rawlins. Have them take a letter to the telegraph office and send word to Cheyenne that we need a judge."

"Might take four or five days to get an answer."

"In the meantime, we'll see what Jesse has to say." Cook peeled a note from the stack of fives. "Go find the undertaker and pay him for the West brothers."

Adam left for the saloon. When he arrived, Lucy was kneeling on the floor, still scrubbing blood from the spot where the West brothers had been murdered.

A tall blonde in a green skirt and a shirtwaist yellow blouse printed with myrtle blossoms slouched against the bar. Her curly hair was pinned up. She straightened, and a smile dimpled her rouged cheeks. "Look at the new deputy."

Out of habit, Adam's attention dropped to her left hand. He noticed the wedding band there. An unaccompanied married woman in the saloon? Maybe he'd found a way to keep busy tonight and ease the heartache that still burned.

He turned to Lucy. "Ma'am, I'm looking for the undertaker."

Lucy paused from her scrubbing and cocked a thumb at the street. "Mister Blair took the bodies to his morgue. Go out the door, turn right, and head down the road toward the cemetery." She rinsed her brush in the bucket and went back to cleaning.

Adam tipped his hat to Lucy and to the woman. She smiled. Then her gaze flicked past his shoulder, and her eyes widened. He turned to look.

Two rough-looking men tramped into the saloon. Flat-brimmed hats shaded savage eyes narrowed to slits. Sharply angled faces looked like leather folded over gristle. Scars crisscrossed their dark cheeks as if they'd been dragged countless times through mesquite. Gnarled hands. Clothes and skin weathered to a uniform brown. Holsters hanging menacingly against their hips.

Adam kept his eyes on the men and whispered to the woman, "You know them?"

She whispered back, "I've never seen them before."

Adam reached for his pistols.

The two men raised their hands, but the mean set of their eyes still burned. One of them said, *"No buscamos pleito."*

Adam palmed the grips of his .45s. *"Que es su negocio aquí?"*

The man on the right wore a handlebar mustache that stretched past his wide cheeks. He appeared to consider Adam's dark complexion and Indian-Mexican features. Then, still in Spanish, he said, "We're looking for Jesse Norman." The mustache stayed stiff when he spoke, like it had been lacquered instead of waxed. Adam decided to name him *Bigotes* . . . Whiskers.

"Por que?" Adam replied.

The men lowered their hands and kept them loose by their sides. Still in Spanish, Bigotes asked, "Is he here?"

"He might be."

"Any chance we can talk to him?"

"You friends of his?"

"Jesse has no friends."

These fellows knew Jesse, all right. Maybe they could answer questions about the big man, the West brothers, and where the money had come from. "Okay, I'll take you to him," Adam said in English. He twirled a finger, signaling the men to turn around. "You go out first. Head across the street to the sheriff's office. Don't give me a reason to use you for target practice."

Neither man replied. Bigotes set his jaw as if swallowing his annoyance. Both men slowly pivoted toward the entrance, then clomped outside onto the wooden sidewalk, heading for the street.

Adam followed them with enough distance to react and shoot. He sized up the men to see which he would shoot first if he had to. As he stepped over the threshold and into the sun, an arm snagged his neck and pulled him off balance. The two men bounded back onto the sidewalk and seized his wrists. He tried to break free, but they held him tight. They dragged him back inside the saloon and pinned him against the bar.

The man who had jumped him relaxed his grip and withdrew a couple of steps. He had a big, stout belly with a bristly face like a feral boar. A full, white beard hung to his collar. Wispy hair dangled from beneath a dirty hat set across a broad forehead burnished by the sun and wind. The expression in his eyes chilled Adam the most. Cold and monstrous . . . like Jesse's.

"By the look on your face," the man growled, "you just

figured out who I am." He nodded. "Hildon Norman. Jesse's older brother. I've come to fetch him."

Hildon pulled Adam's revolvers from their holsters and inspected them. "Very nice." He set them on the counter. "I'll get them later." He brought a thick, dirty finger to Adam's nose. Adam struggled, but the two men held firm with grips like iron.

"Let's play a game, Deputy, so I can learn what kind of a man you are." Hildon tightened his face into a knot of muscle and bone. "First, I'm gonna rip that tin star off your shirt. Then I'm gonna count how many times I have to punch you in the face until you beg me for mercy."

Chapter Eight

Adam wrestled against the two desperados pinning him to the bar. But they held him tight like they were holding down a calf for branding.

He caught a glimpse of Lucy in the corner of his eye as she raced toward the kitchen. She pulled the door open, halted, then backtracked. At gunpoint. Two more outlaws came out of the kitchen, revolvers drawn.

Adam couldn't see behind the bar, but he heard the two gunmen order Lucy to stand next to the strange blonde woman, who muttered curses. He jerked his arms, knowing he couldn't escape, but needing to show he had plenty of fight in him. Even if he managed to pull an arm free and get one of his revolvers, his captors would shoot him full of holes. His only hope for rescue was the sheriff, but Cook was across the street, oblivious to Adam's predicament.

He could stall. Maybe a customer would walk in and shout an alarm.

"If you want your brother," Adam gasped, "let me go, and I can take you to him."

Bigotes reached into his back pocket and pulled out a straight razor. With a flick of his wrist, the blade snapped out, a sliver of light glinting menacingly along its edge.

An ice-cold fear skittered down Adam's spine, and the back of his throat drew tight.

Bigotes grinned as he brought the razor close. "This *lava*

perros told us Jesse is in the sheriff's office across the street."

"I would ask about the West brothers," Hildon grinned and glanced toward the spot—still dark from blood—where they were shot and killed, "but I can see Jesse already found them."

Deep wrinkles creased Hildon's doughy face, and his piggish eyes were drops of dark oil against the whites, tinted the putrid yellow of rancid mayonnaise. "We'll get to Jesse. Can't wait to have him tell me how much he enjoyed killing those double-crossing rats. But first, little Mr. Deputy, let's have some fun with you." He yanked on Adam's shirt, ripping the fabric, but the badge didn't fall.

Bigotes tightened his grip and cooed in Spanish into Adam's ear. "Make it fun for us. Go ahead and start crying, like a *chiquita*." Bigotes waved the razor. "The question is, what do I cut off first? An ear? Your nose? Add them to my collection of mementos?" A leer exposed stained, crooked teeth beneath his hairy lip.

His black eyes cut toward the saloon door. The leer flattened, and his expression cycled from cruel, to surprised, to disappointed, and then to uneasy. He lowered the razor, closed the blade, and slipped the razor into his back pocket. Adam heard the click of pistol hammers, a scuffle of feet, and the rustle of bodies behind the bar.

Sheriff Cook appeared in the entrance. He carried Jesse's Winchester, the rifle aimed at Hildon's back.

Hildon's gaze skipped from man to man. His shoulders sagged, and he turned his head toward Cook. Hildon held still for a moment, then nodded to Bigotes and his partner.

They let go, and Adam slumped against the bar, lightheaded and grateful for the reprieve. He straightened, retrieved his revolvers, and tottered toward Cook, to the cackle of Hildon and his friends.

His face flaming in shame, Adam staggered beside Cook and

drew a pistol. Bigotes and his partner held revolvers trained back at them. The two men behind the bar held Lucy and the blonde woman by the hair and pressed the muzzles of their guns into the women's temples.

Hildon sneered, "Sheriff, there's two of you. Five of us. Think about the odds."

"I know the odds." Cook took a step forward, keeping the Winchester trained on Hildon's belly. "Listen, fatso, anything happens, you die. I get shot, you die. My deputy gets shot, you die. Any of the ladies get shot, you die. Whatever it is you came for won't matter, 'cause you'll be on the floor pissing your pants and bleeding to death."

The expression on Hildon's fat face soured like that of a hog that had found its trough suddenly empty. "I'm not leaving without Jesse."

"He's not going anywhere," Cook replied.

Hildon's eyes smoldered. "I can't leave my kin behind."

"Time you learned how."

The men glared at each other. Flies buzzed around their heads. The wall clock ticked. Adam's pulse beat like a drum.

"This has gone on long enough." The blonde pushed away the barrel of the pistol against her head, startling the gunman. "If you fellows aren't going to do anything but sniff one another's butts like dogs in an alley, let Lucy and me go. We got work to do."

Hildon raised an arm and snapped his fingers. His men shoved the blonde and Lucy out from behind the bar. The two women stumbled across the floor while the men holstered their guns. Hildon strode straight for the saloon door, Bigotes and another outlaw filing behind. Guns at the ready, Cook and Adam stepped aside and let them pass, then followed the next pair of desperados outside.

Five horses tugged at reins lashed to the hitching rail. Six, maybe seven people cowered as they watched from down the street. Hildon climbed onto his horse, a roan mare. His men tethered the Wests' and Jesse's horses to theirs and then mounted up.

Bigotes coaxed his horse close to Adam, looked down at him and spat. "You and me have unfinished business, *cabron.*"

Adam returned the stare. When it came time to kill Bigotes, his first shot would take that wad of waxed hair off the outlaw's lip.

Hildon sat tall in his saddle and scowled. Finally, he snapped his reins, and his horse sprang into the street. His gang circled him, and they rode away in a tornado of hooves and dust.

Adam released the hammer of his pistol. He wished it was as easy to stow his anxiety as it was to holster his gun. A sudden thirst parched his throat. His badge dangled from his torn shirt, reminding him how he'd been caught unawares. He unfastened the badge and pinned it to the other side of his shirt.

Cook set the Winchester on his shoulder. "How much you wanna bet we're going to see them again too soon."

"That's not a bet worth making."

The blonde stepped between them. "Nelson, who were they?"

"Trouble from Missouri, Gloria."

So Cook knew this woman. She looked like a Gloria, and every Gloria Adam had known was a wildcat. She had an even complexion, high cheekbones, a slender jaw, full lips, tiny crinkles in the corners of her green eyes—the kind of face you wouldn't mind greeting every morning.

Cook said to her, "You okay?"

She gathered her loose curls and pinned them in place. "Some mussed hair is nothing to complain about. The wind has done worse."

"And Lucy?"

"Back to scrubbing the floor. The rest of us should be so

diligent." She glanced at Adam. "You okay?"

His wounded pride still smarted. "I'll live."

Cook strode ahead, rifle held loosely at his side, and announced to the scattered crowd in a voice booming with confidence and authority, "Everyone go about their business. I've got this under control." Gloria waved and retreated down the sidewalk, her heels ticking on the wooden planks.

Adam joined Cook in his office. The saddlebags rested on the bench, empty. Adam looked at the safe. "I'm going to need the combination."

Cook twitched his eyebrows and mustache.

Adam read his hesitation and pressed. "What if something happens to you?"

Cook sucked through his teeth. Adam could tell he was thinking of a reason to say no. Apparently, he couldn't. He set the Winchester in the wall rack and pointed to the bookcase. "On the middle shelf. Pull those three volumes out. *The Compendium of Territorial Law.* The combination is written under the shelf."

Adam stoked coals in the stove. The stress from facing down Hildon caught up with him, and his posture flagged. They could both use a cup of hot coffee. Hildon and his gang would be back, and he wondered what Cook intended to do when that happened. "What's your plan when Hildon returns?"

"Not sure. Staying above ground is the least of it."

Adam decided to explore more pleasant thoughts. "What can you tell me about Gloria?"

Cook's head lifted, and Adam sensed a smile. "She's Daryl Anderson's wife. They run the general store."

Adam recalled her defiance. "Tough woman."

"Yep."

And her eyes. And hair. Lips. Bosom. "Attractive woman."

"Yep."

"Seems like good company."

"She is." Cook turned. A grin peeked beneath his mustache.

"What does Mr. Anderson suspect about her social adventures?"

"They seem to have an arrangement. Meaning they pretend not to notice when either of them wanders." Discussing Gloria had definitely brightened Cook's mood. "Get your shirt washed and mended. Lucy can do it."

Or Adam could buy a new shirt. At the general store. Hopefully Gloria would be there, and he'd have a good reason to linger and chat.

Cook took the coffee pot out the front door and dumped the dregs into the street. "Take your time. Get something to eat. A shave. Meanwhile, Jesse and me will have a talk. Figure a way to keep us all alive even if it means him spending a little time in prison."

Adam understood the order to scram. He crossed the street at a diagonal, making for the general store. Wooden barrels and bags of grain sat behind the windows. Bills pasted to the glass panes advertised: *Brush Plow $7.50; Bridle Bits 50¢; Broad Axe $1.25; Worm Syrup $2.15; Muslin Drawers 45¢; Lard 10 lbs. 70¢.*

A bell tinkled above the door as he entered. With merchandise stacked floor to rafters, the general store looked like every other mercantile he'd been in. But compared to the desolation and drabness surrounding the town, all these goods and trinkets beckoned like heavenly treasures.

A wide door at the back opened into another room. A tall, lanky man emerged and wiped his hands on a denim apron as he apologized for not answering promptly. Tufts of pale hair feathered over his large ears, and a clerk's green visor cast a shadow over his eyes. A tidy mustache wiggled under his long nose, giving the impression of a friendly rodent. Adam recognized the proprietor as Daryl Anderson, from their earlier introduction at the saloon.

Daryl beamed a How-Much-Are-You-Willing-to-Spend smile. He noticed Adam's deputy badge and shared details of the confrontation with Hildon from what his wife had told him. Adam asked about her and said he wanted to apologize for the disrespect she had suffered at the hands of such rough criminals.

Daryl laughed. "Before I married Gloria, she'd been taken hostage by the Cheyenne. After two days, they returned her to an outpost. It takes more than gun-happy scum to ruffle her feathers."

Adam wanted to see her but didn't want to push too hard. He asked for a new shirt, and Daryl offered a checked outing shirt for only two dollars. Recalling how much the sheriff liked his coffee, Adam asked for a dollar's worth, three pounds. Daryl placed the shirt and the bag of coffee in a large paper sack. Adam paid with a five.

Daryl straightened like he had something important to announce. "I'm sure Sheriff Cook informed you that I publish the local newspaper, *The Luther Ledger*."

Adam shook his head. "He didn't mention it."

"What happened back in the saloon will make for an especially rich piece of journalism," Daryl said. "How about you give me your version of events?" He cocked an eyebrow. "Add some color to the article."

"Sure," Adam replied, flattered. This publicity might bring Gloria around, asking for more details about him.

Daryl invited him to the back room, going on and on about the lawlessness of modern society. Whenever he used a big word like "degenerate," "odious," and "reprobates," he would stop to see if he'd lost Adam.

The back room was as large as the front room and just as packed with goods. Daryl explained, "Given my other duties, I try to publish twice a month, and, if the occasion warrants it, I publish a special edition just like the big city papers." As he spoke, Daryl led Adam to a corner with a strong solvent odor. A type box and a printing press stood beside shelves stacked with paper and cans of ink.

He showed Adam the paper cutter. It was a metal table with a vise to hold down a thick pad of paper. After adjusting the vise to size the cut, he grasped a long iron lever above his head, set his weight on it and yanked down. A guillotine blade dropped along the face of the vise and cut the paper with a satisfying muffled *thwack*.

He let go of the lever, and it swung upwards. "Can't tell you how many times this machine has paid for itself. I can cut a hundred sheets at a time in any size. People need handbills, I can make them. If women need stationery for letters, it's no problem." Daryl picked up the paper he had cut and set it aside on a stool.

The front bell tinkled. A woman asked for Daryl in a singsong voice and inquired if her canning supplies had arrived. He asked Adam to wait and went back to the front room.

Adam set the sack with his shirt and coffee on a table and wandered among the supplies. He could have made plenty selling this stuff in the lean years after the war, when everything was scarce except for hunger and cripples.

What wasn't scarce was the cash Cook had locked in his safe. Thirty-four thousand, five hundred dollars. Cook had already given him a nice chunk, but it would be a shame not to keep a bigger share. What if the sheriff decided to return it all? How could Adam take some of the money without revealing that he had?

Circling back to Daryl's printing equipment, Adam stared at the paper cutter. And stared.

Chapter Nine

Quietly, Adam side-stepped to the storeroom door. Daryl was busy helping his customer gather goods in a crate.

Adam returned to the paper cutter. He reached into a shirt pocket for his leather wallet and pulled out a dollar bill. He flattened the bill on the cutter table and measured its length against the paper under the vise bar. He could cut three equal lengths with an inch or two left over. He took a moment to remember what he'd watched Daryl do, then loosened the wheel that pressed the vise bar onto the pad of paper. After repositioning the paper to match the width of the dollar note, he screwed the wheel tight.

He paused to listen for Daryl. Still chatting with the customer.

Adam grasped the handle of the cutting lever, pulled with all his weight, and sliced a stack of paper. Worried that he might have been heard, he checked on Daryl. The grocer seemed more interested in talking and flirting than filling his customer's order.

Back to work. Adam cut another two stacks. He aligned all three stacks side by side and cut them to size lengthwise. Then he slid the remaining paper forward and made two more cuts. Now he had nine stacks, each the size of a brick of money. He placed the paper in the sack with his new shirt and coffee and arranged the paper cutter to look as if it hadn't been disturbed.

One more thing. He would need glue. He rummaged through the shelves, found a box with small bottles of leather cement, and dropped one in the sack.

Back in the store proper, he introduced himself to the customer and got waylaid by Daryl, who ran on about how Adam and Cook had chased the Hildon gang out of town. "You'll read all about it in my newspaper," Daryl said.

The customer—a big-hipped woman with a braid the size of a horse's tail—beamed appreciatively and promised Adam a jar of her canned peaches in gratitude for his brave service. He thanked her and, on the way out, thought to ask Daryl, "Two more items. A bottle of whiskey and tincture of laudanum."

Daryl didn't sell whiskey, but he offered a pint bottle of medicinal brandy, 60 proof. Fifty cents. *Good enough.* He added a tiny, quarter-ounce phial of laudanum, and Adam slipped both in the sack.

"You promised me an interview," Daryl said, then added as he turned to the woman, "for my newspaper."

"Absolutely. Soon as we're both free," Adam replied, though he noticed that Daryl kept his attention on the woman.

Adam left the store and walked across the street. He detoured behind the sheriff's office, where he hid the cut stacks of paper in the hay crib until the opportunity arose to try his plan.

He proceeded to the Mountain View Saloon and Hotel, where he got a meal and a shave from Lucy and changed into his new shirt while he left the torn one for her to wash and mend. With his badge pinned in place, he returned to the sheriff's office and set the sack with the brandy and the laudanum on a corner of the shelf. He found Cook slouching in a chair in the back room, hatless, gumming the butt of a cigar, hands hooked into the belt loops of his trousers, his boots crossed at the ankles. A film of smoke dirtied the air. Jesse sat on his bunk in the jail cell, drawing on a cheroot, the bruises on his face the color of raspberries.

The killer and Cook looked at each other, grim faced, puffing like they were trading smoke signals. Cook uncrossed his ankles, stood, and said to Adam, " 'Bout goddamn time you got here."

Adam showed him the coffee.

Cook smiled in appreciation. He grabbed his hat from a wall peg. "The place is yours. I'll be gone for a few hours." He dropped his cigar butt into a bucket and stomped out with the Winchester.

Adam waited until the front door closed. He returned to the front office and peeked past the window curtain, watching the sheriff disappear into the saloon. Then he glanced up and down the street, making certain no one approached. He withdrew the brandy and the laudanum from the sack, opened the bottle and the vial, and trickled laudanum into the brandy. *Careful.* He didn't want to poison Jesse.

He measured out half of the tincture and recorked both bottles. He tucked the laudanum into his trouser pocket and shook the brandy bottle, then he slipped it back into the paper sack and returned to the jail.

Jesse remained on the bed, placid as a bull chewing its cud, biding its time. Adam walked up to the cell and leaned against the bars. "What did you and the sheriff talk about?"

Jesse examined the ember of his cigar. "Nothin' much. Mostly how the two of you should go rot in hell."

"Shame." Adam pulled the brandy from the sack. "I brought something for your aches."

Jesse shrugged.

Adam tossed the bottle between the bars. Jesse easily snatched it midair. He studied the label and, with great effort, mouthed the words. He uncapped the bottle and sniffed. One eyebrow arched in suspicion. "What's the deal?"

"You don't want it, give it back."

Jesse took a brief sip, swished it, then swallowed. "It'll do. Doesn't mean you shouldn't go to hell." He cradled the opened bottle against his chest, lifted his feet onto the cot, and rested against the wall. "Much obliged. Time comes for me to kill you, I'll make it quick."

Adam made sure the back door was barred properly and returned to the office, where he set a kettle to boil on the stove. The empty saddlebags lay against the wall under the rifle rack. He went out to fetch the paper he had left in the hay crib. Back in the office, he placed his gun belt on the desk, then crouched by the bookcase. He slid the three volumes of the *Compendium* from the shelf. The safe combination was where Cook said it would be, under the shelf above the books.

He memorized the numbers and returned to the desk, where he picked through the gazettes and the broadsheets, and watched the clock. When a half hour had passed, he checked on Jesse. The hairy giant was lying on his side. Snoring. Boots off. Feet in dirty socks pointed toward the cell door. The empty bottle of brandy lay on the floor beneath the cot.

Adam went back to the office and opened the safe. He felt like Ali Baba entering the thieves' den. The bricks of money looked fewer in number than before. He counted and sure enough, five were missing. Three of twenties and two of tens. Eight thousand dollars.

Den of thieves was right, *Sheriff Nelson Cook.*

The kettle boiled.

He took a brick of twenties and passed it through the plume of steam until the glue holding the paper band dissolved. The band separated, and the brick came loose in his hand. Adam's heart beat faster. What if Cook stepped through the door? So what if he did? It wasn't like the sheriff could argue his own purity of heart. He and Adam would just have to negotiate how to split their respective takes.

Adam steamed eight more bricks. He replaced the bills in the first brick of twenties with paper, leaving a few notes on the top and bottom. After setting the brick on the desk, he repeated the procedure with another brick, then another, until he'd replaced money from nine bricks. He spread a dab of leather cement on the paper band around the first brick and held it in place until the cement took. The band wasn't anywhere as snug as it should be, and the discolored spot on the paper might invite a close inspection, but, for now, it was good enough. He re-glued the bands on the rest of the bricks and took a moment to admire his handiwork before returning them to the safe.

Two bricks of twenties. Four thousand dollars.

Five bricks of tens. Five thousand dollars.

Two bricks of fives. One thousand dollars.

He put the altered bricks under the other money in the safe to better disguise what he'd done. Next, he rummaged through the office cupboard and plucked an empty flour sack from a heap in the lower cabinet, then gathered the loose money in the sack. Where to hide the cash? He thought about the hay crib but worried someone might find it.

He checked on Jesse again. The big man was in such a deep drunken slumber, a train crashing into the jail wouldn't waken him.

Back in the office, Adam glanced around the room. He needed a place he could get to but not a place Cook would ever stumble across. Searching behind and around the furniture, he discovered loose, uneven floorboards peeking out from under the bookcase. He emptied the bookcase and scooted it forward, then pried up the loosest board to reveal a shallow crawlspace.

He hefted the sack. *Ten thousand dollars.* Minus the notes he had sandwiched around the bricks to give the illusion the money was all there. He doubted he'd ever get an opportunity to score this much money again.

Then why not leave now? Take advantage of his good fortune while he could.

Guilt needled his heart.

Because Cook needed him. Hildon Norman and his gang would be back, and, of all the underhanded tricks Adam had played in his life, he had yet to leave a buddy facing the enemy alone. Call him a womanizer, thief, scoundrel, cheat . . . anything but a coward. Deserting a comrade would hurt worse than catching a bullet in the belly. Tess and her snooty family had never understood that kind of honor.

He bade the money goodbye and dropped it into the hole, followed by the bottle of leather cement. He emptied what was left of the laudanum and discarded the phial. Retrieving the money would be a challenge for another day. He used the butt of the Spencer carbine to tap the loose floorboard back into place, replaced the bookcase and books, and burned the remaining slips of cut blank paper. Last, he scanned the room to make sure nothing looked out of place.

The sun sank behind the saloon across the street, and a dusky veil fell across the office window. Adam plopped into Cook's chair and massaged a cramp in his neck, relieved and surprised he'd managed to swap the paper for the money without getting caught. The room darkened, so he fired an oil lamp and hung it from a hook above the desk and placed his gun belt and hat under the bench. In the bookcase he found *A Lost History of the Noble Race*. He lay down on the bench, one pistol tucked by his side, and tried to read.

His mind drifted to what life would be like if he managed to escape with the money. Say goodbye to Luther, Wyoming. Most likely head to Tucson or San Francisco. Maybe back to New Orleans. Definitely stay clear of St. Louis.

Return to the Comancheria? And do what? Rustle cattle? Horses?

Thoughts of women percolated in his memory. He'd known a good number of ladies and was plenty cynical about romance and true love. *Bedding married women will do that to you.*

And then there was Tess. Not married but still plenty off limits. She was white and well bred. It figured she was the one who turned him away. Because her father said Adam didn't have enough schooling. Or property. What he didn't say, but what lay at the heart of his objections, was that she couldn't marry a Mexican half-breed. Three different ways of saying Adam wasn't good enough no matter how well he'd educated himself or acquitted himself in service to his country.

Adam tapped the slim leather wallet in his breast pocket, behind his deputy sheriff's badge. He kept a letter—*Tess's letter*—in the wallet so he could carry it against his person yet not ruin it with his sweat. Maybe soon he could go East and call on her again. Ten thousand dollars would go a long way to making him look like a respectable man, even if he wasn't Anglo.

The room cooled. He shoved more wood into the stove, enjoying its warmth as he remembered all the times he'd been wet, cold, and miserable.

Cook returned at nine, smelling of peppered sausage, whiskey, and tobacco smoke. He carried a saucepan covered with a lid. "Brought you stew."

Adam thanked him and placed the warm pan on his lap. He removed the lid to reveal hunks of bread floating on top of the stew. Cook gave him a fork to spear the meat and vegetables before readying a fresh pot of coffee and lighting a cigar. "How's our prisoner?"

"Sleeping. Gave him brandy to shut his mouth."

"Brandy? Mighty generous of you. If I could get away with it, I'd poison him with two slugs of hot lead. Anyway, while I was eating dinner, I made up my mind about what we're going to do with him."

Adam sopped stew with the bread. "What's that?"

Cook claimed the chair behind his desk, where he savored his cigar and the lingering whiskey buzz. "The stage arrives tomorrow afternoon. When it leaves for Rawlins the next morning, I'm sending you and Jesse along. That way we only have tonight to watch him. If Hildon wants his brother back, let him take on the marshal and the army."

"What about the money?"

"Sign it over to Wells Fargo. Let the stage take it."

Adam's guts knotted. When the bricks got inventoried, his deception would be discovered for certain.

Cook got up to check on Jesse. He returned to his desk and placed the Winchester within quick reach, then sat back down and planted his boots on the desk. "Adam, you want to sleep, go ahead. I'll take the first watch."

"You sure? I'm plenty rested."

"You want to stay awake, that's your business." Cook opened a desk drawer and pulled out a copy of *The National Police Gazette*. The scantily clad beauty on the cover clutched her breast and stared upward as if praying, *Forgive me, Father, for I have sinned.*

Adam loosened his shirt and trouser belt but kept his boots on. Instead of counting sheep, he wondered what lies he could tell if asked about the faked money.

The next thing he knew, Cook shook him awake and shushed him. Blinking, Adam sat up and rubbed his eyes. The lamp was out, and the room was as gloomy as a cave, save for the flickering glow leaking from the stove. Cook palmed the Winchester.

Dogs barked. Close by, a horse neighed. It couldn't belong to Adam or Cook. Their horses were stabled at the blacksmith's.

Adam reached for his gun belt and quietly buckled it on. Flecks of orange from the stove's embers sparkled over the butts of his shiny Colt revolvers.

Something banged against the eaves.

Adam gulped, his mouth dry, pulse quickening. He pictured Hildon and Bigotes and the rest of their gang outside like pumas stalking a barn full of livestock.

Wood creaked. It sounded like someone climbing a ladder.

Footfalls on the roof. Adam cocked his pistol and followed the noise.

More creaking of the ladder. More footfalls.

Adam looked to Cook for guidance. The sheriff panned the Winchester in search of a target.

Gunshots blasted from above, and bullets ripped through the ceiling. Dozens of slugs. A torrent of slugs. From pistols. Rifles. Shotguns.

Adam and Cook scrambled against the walls as wood splintered around them. They emptied their guns at the ceiling, firing wildly, the muzzle blasts dazzling, the reports deafening.

Cook lunged to the front door. The instant he opened it, a volley of bullets tore through the wood. He slammed the door and dug into his pockets for shells to reload the Winchester. The gun smoke was so thick both men coughed.

Between the hammering of gunshots, something sizzled, buzzing like the tail of an angry rattlesnake. A trail of sparks dropped from the ceiling right over their heads. Horrified, Adam saw what they'd come from.

The fuse on a small keg of gunpowder.

Chapter Ten

Adam flung the bench on its side and dove behind it, eyes shut tight, hands flat against his ears.

The keg bounced on the floor, rolled, and exploded.

Hot air slapped his face. Stung his nostrils. The floor shuddered beneath him, and the bench slammed him into the wall.

Adam lay still, stunned.

Eyes closed, hands still clamped to his ears, he felt the vibration of feet stamping across the floor. Things sliding. Tearing apart.

Smoke clogged his nostrils. Coughing, he opened his eyes, saw nothing but darkness, snatched a revolver from his holster, and pointed the gun upward.

Heart pounding, he remained still, thumb poised on the pistol hammer. Worked spit into his mouth. He remained still, not sure if the gang outside waited for him to move.

Horses whinnied. Wheels creaked. Men cursed in muffled voices. Hooves stamped the ground, and a wagon rumbled over the hard dirt, the sounds finding a percussive rhythm, rising to a raucous crescendo, then the hoofbeats and wagon wheels faded to silence.

Slowly, Adam raised his head and peered over the bench to survey the damage. Moonlight poured through the front window, past ragged shards of glass that clung to the sash like broken teeth. The remnants of the window curtain hung from one side, and orange embers laced the smoldering cloth. Curls of smoke and motes of ash swirled through holes blasted in the ceiling.

He sat up and ran a clammy hand over his face. As his eyes adjusted to the gloom, he took in the discouraging details. The overhead lantern was gone. Debris—paper, bits of glass, the shattered clock, splinters of wood—littered the floor. The blast had stripped the walls bare. Cook's desk leaned against the bookcase like the carcass of a slain bull.

Sheriff Cook lay between the desk and the front door. His boots moved, and he stirred, rising mechanically until he propped himself on his arms. Miraculously, he still wore his derby.

Grateful that his friend was alive, Adam stood and stepped over the bench to grasp Cook's hand and help him up. Cook groped the floor for the Winchester and rose to his full height. He repeatedly shut his eyes and opened them. He and Adam stared at each other, too numb to speak.

Finally, Adam asked, "You hurt?"

Cook shouted, "What?"

Adam repeated the question, louder this time.

Cook rubbed his ear. "Got the blast still ringing in my head." He abruptly noticed the burning curtain, snatched it, and threw it to the floor, where he ground the embers under his boot.

They inspected the room. Two parallel scrape marks on the floor ran from the front wall and through the rear doorway into the jail.

Hildon and his raiders had taken the safe through the back door. Not surprisingly, the jail cell was open, the key still in the lock. Jesse was gone. Adam glanced around. The saddlebags were also gone.

The back door to the building was missing. Adam stepped out. A three-quarters moon illuminated the landscape in silvery light. The door lay by the horse trough. A pair of ropes stretched from the door across the dirt. The back of the office faced an empty lot bordered by a row of sheds. Beyond that, miles of empty Wyoming.

Drawn by an approaching commotion, Adam and Cook walked back through the jail, the office, and emerged out the front door. Candles and lamps shone in windows up and down the street. From the south, a procession of men approached with lanterns held aloft.

The man in front hollered in a deep voice that gave him away. Burt Rex, the blacksmith. "Hello, Sheriff. You all right?"

"We're okay. More or less," Adam shouted back.

The group marched closer, a tight herd of men clutching rifles and shotguns. Pistols jutted from waist belts. Light shining on their faces reflected anxiety and fear.

"We heard the shooting and the explosion," Rex said, his teeth shining between his dense mustache and thick beard. He held a barn lantern in one hand, a double-barreled goose gun in the other. As the biggest man in town, people tended to regard him as a leader, though by the unease in his eyes, he didn't welcome the responsibility.

The men lined up around the spread of broken glass in the street. Lantern light shimmered across the shattered pieces.

"My Percheron is missing," Rex lamented. "Plus my buckboard."

"Who was it, Sheriff?" asked one of the other townsmen. He nervously fingered the action of his rifle. "The men you ran into earlier? Hildon Norman and his criminals?"

"Looks like it," Adam replied.

He and Cook returned to the office. Rex and a couple of the other men followed. The rest remained outside in fretful vigilance.

Now that the shock of the explosion had receded, Adam felt a blush of shame. He and Cook represented the law. People were supposed to respect—and fear—them. Instead, their stronghold had been reduced to shambles in an attack that left them cowering on the floor.

Rex studied the splintered back doorframe where the hinges and latch had been ripped free. "That explains why they took Thor. They needed a draft horse to pull the door clean off." The blacksmith stepped outside. He swept a lantern to illuminate the ground. "Why did they take the wagon?"

Adam pointed to the parallel marks on the floor. "To steal the safe." He had to admit being impressed by the thoroughness of the plan to rescue Jesse and steal back the loot. But what would happen when the Normans opened the safe and discovered they'd been hoodwinked?

Cook pressed a folded handkerchief to his right ear. "Not much to do until daylight," he shouted, like everyone else was also hard of hearing. "Rex, gather men for a posse. Meet in front of my office. Eight o'clock."

Cook sent the men home. By the light of a borrowed lantern, he and Adam collected debris and straightened the front room. After several minutes, Cook set his chair upright and slumped into it, appearing not just tired but haggard, spent. He wheezed and coughed up blood.

The sight disturbed Adam. He was familiar with injuries caused by an explosion. During the war, a shell had crashed into a nearby dugout and detonated. The survivors staggered into the open, blood trickling from their ears and noses. Like Cook just now, they began to cough up blood. At first they tried to remain on their feet, but after an hour they lay on the ground wheezing and coughing until they died. A surgeon later told Adam that the shell's explosion had fried and mashed their lungs. Adam prayed Cook would be okay.

At sunup, Lucy brought coffee, eggs, and biscuits. Cook barely sipped the coffee and instead drank a lot of cold water.

Adam ate his fill. After breakfast, he cleaned and reloaded one of his pistols, then the other. He put fresh rounds in the empty loops of his gun belt.

Cook dabbed his ear with a fresh handkerchief. It came away spotted with blood.

Adam said, "Gonna be all right?"

Cook chuffed. "Hell, no," he shouted. "Even if my hearing completely returns, I won't be okay until I see the Norman brothers and the rest of those ill-bred sons-of-whores swing from the gallows while ravens peck at their eyes." He tore a biscuit and nibbled on it. At least his appetite was returning.

"Feel pretty strongly about this, Sheriff?"

"I advise you do the same. You get the chance, show them no mercy."

Shortly after eight, Rex and a posse of four men arrived on horseback. They looked exactly like what they were: family men anxious over their homes. A couple of the riders towed horses behind them, Adam's roan and what had to be Cook's mount, both stabled at Rex's.

Cook briefed the men that they would follow the wagon tracks as far as possible. "They wander off the trail, they risk bustin' a wheel."

One of the others chimed in. "What's in the safe?"

"Money recovered from the two fellas that were killed in the saloon yesterday."

Adam looked away, embarrassed by the truth.

"Figure they're going to blow it open?" a rider asked.

"Won't do much good," Cook replied. "The gunpowder it would take would also burn up what's inside. So they have to keep dragging it until they can get to a place where they can drill the lock. But they can't do that anywhere close by." He checked to make sure everyone had water and ammunition and told them to remain alert.

He and Adam mounted up. Cook carried the Winchester, Adam the Spencer repeater.

The men filed behind them, none looking too eager. If Cook called off the posse, Adam doubted any of them would've been disappointed.

They took the main road north. Townspeople watched from the sidewalks, their eyes heavy with anxiety and fear, as the posse departed. A quarter mile out of town, the road narrowed to a trail not much wider than stagecoach ruts, and it cut across the lowest ground between the rugged hills.

Cook halted the party. They studied the tracks. The freshest marks no doubt belonged to the Norman gang.

Cook dabbed his ear. It had quit bleeding, so he stuffed the handkerchief inside his vest. "Whaddaya think?" he said, to no one in particular.

Adam pointed with the Spencer. "Seven horses. Plus a big one pulling the wagon."

"That's Thor," Rex reminded them. "Hope nothing happened to him. He's a good horse and cost me plenty."

Adam advanced to take point. Another rider pulled behind him and rode to the right, head up and scanning the horizon, cradling a shotgun like he had military experience.

An hour passed. Then another. Dust puffed beneath the horses' hooves. The sun hovered over the tallest hills and beamed with growing ferocity. Heat and boredom sapped their wariness.

Adam wondered what the Normans would do when they learned they'd stolen stacks of worthless paper amid the rest of the money. Might they double back and attack Luther out of revenge? The stoutest of the townsmen were here on the trail, so there was nothing to stop the Norman gang from pillaging the place. With every passing minute, a steady drip of pessimism soured Adam's thoughts.

Up ahead, behind shrubs clustered on a low mound ... movement. A horse's head appeared. Adam's mind snapped to attention. He readied the Spencer and glanced back at the rider behind him, making sure the fellow was alert. The rider nodded and hitched his shoulders, then cocked back the hammers of his shotgun.

Adam gazed along the high ground, looking for anyone waiting in ambush. The hills rose in steps from the trail, terraces of thick shrub and steep rock. Horses couldn't climb the incline except slowly and in single file between the outcroppings. He scrutinized every shadow beneath the bushes or in the rocky folds. Only songbirds fluttered around him, a comforting sign that told him danger had long passed.

He waved to Cook. The sheriff waved back and motioned for the remainder of the posse to fan out. Adam led his horse off the trail and to the left of the wooded mound.

On the reverse side, an enormous draft horse stood in a draw behind the mound. Rex's Percheron, harnessed to a wagon. Ears twitching, it calmly munched on buffalo grass, as if knowing someone would eventually come along.

The buckboard rested at an angle. The left front wheel was crooked and looked about to work loose. The safe, Hildon's prize, lay in the middle of the wagon bed, on its back, its door open.

Cook and the posse closed around Adam. Rex brightened when he saw the big, gray Percheron. He started to ride toward it, but Adam whispered, "Hold still."

Cook signaled for the other riders to scout the periphery of the draw. He nodded to Adam, who hid a nervous gulp, worried that his swindle would be exposed.

After getting the all clear, they rode close to the wagon. Loose papers and envelopes—the sheriff's official documents—lay like trash in the wagon bed. The safe was empty.

Adam had expected to see his fake money scattered everywhere. But it was gone, along with the saddlebags.

Cook scoped the ground. A lantern lay in the dirt beside the wagon. "Here's what I surmise. One of the gang must've been a safe cracker. They had to stop to open the safe soon as the wheel gave out."

Adam turned from Cook to hide the relief spilling across his face. He imagined what had happened. Working in the dark, the outlaws had been in a hurry to open the safe, and, once they figured the combination, were too rushed to examine the money. Just a quick glance under lamplight—with cackles of triumph—and then they'd stuffed the bricks of cash into the saddlebags. His theft remained undiscovered for the moment.

Rex dismounted and inspected the wagon. "I can fix the wheel enough to drive it back into town. Nothing much lost except time."

One of the riders asked, "What now?"

Cook squinted in the direction the hoofprints led, straight through the wooded hills. His eyes were still bloodshot. "Now that they're not pulling the wagon, they're putting plenty of distance between us and them. No point chasing men who have nothing to lose."

The posse replied with a collective nod.

Adam and two of the men helped right the wagon while Rex kicked the wheel back into position. Cook collected his papers. Rex got on his other horse and grasped Thor's reins to lead the big animal back to Luther.

Back in town, Cook ordered the posse to carry the safe into his office and then thanked them for their service. Though they weren't paid, they had all returned without any bullets in their persons. He gave Adam ten dollars and told him to get with Daryl Anderson, start making arrangements to repair the office and jail. Adam ran the errand, then stopped by the saloon for a meal and a shave.

When he returned to the office, Cook had rustled up clean writing paper plus pen and ink from someplace and had written five complete pages. He folded the papers into an envelope and wrote on the front of it. "This is my official account about what happened here. The stage should be arriving soon, and, when it leaves tomorrow, I want you to accompany it to Rawlins. Give this to the marshal." He handed the envelope to Adam. "I'll leave it up to him to handle the Normans and Hildon's pack of devils."

Rex and a crew of men and boys arrived. A couple of them climbed on the roof to fix the bullet holes and broken planks where the gunpowder keg had dropped through, while Rex and a carpenter repaired the back door. Adam and a boy plastered holes in the office and jail walls. Cook didn't do much except sit in his chair. He lit a cigar and tried a puff, then clutched his chest, coughed, and grimaced painfully. He squashed the cigar into an ashtray as his complexion turned a pale green. After sips of water, his face returned to its normal color.

Late in the afternoon, Cook dismissed the work crew. Lucy brought hot food for the sheriff and Adam. The warm meal soothed Adam's nerves and made him appreciate that, once again, he had cheated death.

Shouting broke the tranquil mood. Adam swallowed the last morsel of pork. A hunch told him the shouting did not herald good news. He wiped his mouth and walked out of the office.

A woman on a pony galloped down the street. A hat fluttered behind her neck, held in place by a neck cinch. She jerked her pony to a halt in front of the sheriff's office. With a very unladylike throw of a leg, she swung off the saddle and planted her boots in the dirt. Both she and the pony heaved deep breaths. Sweat lathered along its harness and saddle.

The newcomer wore men's denim riding britches, a leather

vest, and a dingy white blouse over her compact frame, looking not so much dirty as wild and untamed. Sweat and grime mottled her face. Small, blue eyes sparked with excitement and alarm. She plucked off her hat, revealing dull, black hair gathered into a loose bun.

Cook, coming up next to Adam, stared at her. "Now who might you be?"

Still gasping for breath, the woman ignored him and turned back to her horse. With what seemed like great urgency, she untied the saddlebags hitched behind her saddle, then lifted the bags and tossed them. They landed with a thud on the wooden sidewalk.

Adam felt light-headed when he recognized the bags. The same ones at the center of all this trouble. The bags looked full. And most certainly with his fake money.

Chapter Eleven

"My name is Francine Mills," the woman said. Grime darkened the wrinkles at the corners of her eyes, making her look older than she likely was. Adam guessed between sixteen and nineteen. When she shifted her weight from foot to foot, the motion parted her vest and revealed the butt of a small revolver tucked into her pants.

Cook noted the diminutive gun, then dropped his gaze to the saddlebags. "I don't suppose I have to ask you what's in those."

Adam tamped the queasiness creeping up his throat. "The question is, how?"

"How?" Francine repeated. She blinked at him, as if his question made no sense.

"The money," Adam elaborated. "How'd you get it?"

"I've been riding with Brandon Carruthers—"

Cook raised his hand. "Hold on. Brandon Carruthers? Not the Normans?"

"Hildon Norman joined up with Carruthers," the girl explained.

Cook's face went pale.

"What's the problem?" Adam asked, as if going against the Normans wasn't bad enough.

"Brandon Carruthers is the Silver Fox," Cook replied.

Adam didn't need to hear more. The Silver Fox was legend, an outlaw whose reputation bordered on myth. Thief. Robber. Murderer. A villain so ghostly it was easy to believe he was more phantom than flesh and blood. But he was a real man with a real name, and now his bloody shadow fell over Luther.

Cook asked, "What were you doing with those outlaws?"

Francine took a deep breath. "Minding their camp." Slow and soft at first, the tenor of her voice sharpened as she continued. "They were washing up in a creek. I was supposed to be cooking when I took the money."

"The Silver Fox let you walk away with all this cash? They didn't chase you?"

"I scattered their horses."

"You know Carruthers and Hildon Norman aren't going to let you get away with this."

Francine curled her lip into a snarl. She rested a hand on the butt of the revolver. "I had no choice. Kevin West was my man. They killed him, so I'm getting back at them the best way I know how." She kicked the saddlebags.

Adam clasped Cook's arm and herded him close to the office wall. "Won't be long before the Silver Fox and his gang come looking for her and the money," he whispered.

"So what if he does?" Cook flexed his shoulders and straightened his badge.

"We barely survived the Normans' last visit."

"This time we know what to expect, don't we?" Cook narrowed his eyes and stared down the street, projecting an appearance that was mean and protective. He pointed to the townspeople who'd gathered along the street, inching closer as the minutes passed. "See that? That look we're getting. The look of fear. The look that says I might not be up to my job of keeping the peace. It's a look I don't like."

Adam couldn't deny the apprehension in the townsfolk's faces. "What are you going to do about it?"

"Lock up the woman and keep her from getting into more trouble. Safeguard the money. Tomorrow you ride with the stage to Rawlins. Give my letter to the marshal. After you get back, we'll leave with a tracking party to find Carruthers."

"Wouldn't it make more sense for me to stay with you? I can give your report to the stage driver. He can deliver it to the marshal."

Cook kept his gaze on something faraway. "What I need is for you to follow my instructions."

"I appreciate what you're trying to prove, Nelson."

"You mean Sheriff Cook."

Adam held his breath, then let it out in a long sigh. *"Sheriff."* A pause. "You're going to need me here. Why not put—" He stopped himself. He was going to say Cook should put the money and Francine on the stage, and he would ride escort. But if that happened, the stagecoach driver would demand an accounting of the money, and the cut-up paper would be discovered. Adam felt an all too familiar unease return.

Cook finished the sentence. "You mean put the woman and the money on the stage?"

"I didn't say anything."

"But you were going to." Cook shook his head. "I'm not going to export my problems. And I can't risk putting the stage in danger. Better that Miss Mills and the money stay here." He patted his vest, found a cigar, and brought it to his lips. Finally, he looked at Adam. "You gonna keep bothering me about this, or do I have to appoint a new deputy?"

Adam backed away, hands raised. "You are the boss. I hear, and I obey."

Cook repressed a grin. "That would be a first, you slick bastard." He turned back to Francine, who was hitching her pony to a post. "Let's see what's in the bags."

She crouched and opened one bag's flap. The top edges of the bricks of cash peeked out. Adam's heart sank. Tens and twenties.

"The money's all here," she said.

The fake money, anyway. If anyone found out about his ruse, people would start asking questions. Carruthers and Hildon Norman had no reason to make the switch. When they had the money, wouldn't they try and get away as fast as possible? Suspicions might swirl around Adam. Why was he in Luther? What was he running from? He was no bank robber, but he was the kind of man who'd skim the cream of easy takings. Daryl Anderson might notice some of his paper missing and recall that Adam had the opportunity to use his paper cutter. The storekeeper had even shown him how. Adam closed his eyes. The ground swayed beneath his feet.

He wanted Cook to reach down and take a stack of money, inspect it, and learn that it was a trick. End the charade and set his heart at ease.

Instead Cook ordered, "Bring the bags inside." He thumped Adam's chest. "Be a gentleman and help the lady."

Adam toted the bags into the office. They felt heavy, like guilt.

Cook opened the safe. "Stash them here."

Adam crammed the saddlebags inside. Cook shut the front and spun the tumbler.

"What about me?" Francine asked, as if she expected praise for her act of theft. She dropped her hat upside down on the sheriff's desk and raked a hand through her hair.

Cook pointed to the jail. "In there."

"What?"

"You want to see how long you'd last in the open with that pop gun?" He motioned toward her revolver. "Do it my way, and you just might live to see next week."

Shoulders drooping, she stepped toward the back room. Cook held his arm up to stop her. "First the gun, and then empty your pockets."

Francine slipped the pistol—a Smith & Wesson .22—from her waistband and dropped it into her hat. She dug into her pockets and tossed a jackknife and small coins beside the revolver.

Cook grasped the key ring from the wall. "Now get in the cell." He turned to Adam. "You go put the word out in the saloon, the mercantile, and with the blacksmith that I'm going to need men to stand guard with us tonight."

Adam made his rounds as Cook directed. He embellished the call to civic duty by saying that the men in Carruthers's gang most certainly had significant rewards on their heads. He didn't know if this was true, but it sounded reasonable and got him volunteers.

While Adam made his way back to the sheriff's office, the coach from the Cheyenne and Blackhills Stage Line rumbled into town, a small crowd trailing after it like a litter of hungry puppies. The afternoon shadows pulled low across the street, and the air cooled.

The stagecoach halted in front of the saloon, where the driver, the courier guard, and three passengers dismounted. The driver and the guard unloaded luggage and parcels, then climbed back on the stage and drove it to the blacksmith's to stable the horses for the night.

Cook appeared in his office door. He told Adam to watch Francine while he went to the saloon to greet the stage passengers and trade news. Adam found Francine asleep on the cell bunk, curled beneath a blanket.

Twilight settled over the town. Cook returned, and, shortly afterwards, the first volunteer guards arrived. Adam organized the watch. He posted three men with rifles to observe the street from a hotel window above the saloon. After that, he climbed onto the office roof with another pair of men, and they stood vigil, guns loaded and ready. As the night progressed, the town grew silent, and the windows darkened as if the buildings themselves had gone to sleep. Moonlight bleached the ground to a pale gray.

The second shift arrived at two in the morning. The men draped blankets over their shoulders and kept warm by smoking cigars, drinking coffee until that got stale, and switching to pulls of whiskey. At the end of a fretful and uneventful night, Adam met the sunrise with sleepy eyes. He sent the men home, climbed down, and entered the office.

Cook sat in his desk chair, trying to appear alert, but his bleary eyes brimmed over heavy bags beneath. Two days' worth of growth shaded his jowls, and a ragged mustached drooped over his mouth. He blinked until his eyes brightened. A rumpled handkerchief spotted with blood lay on his desk. The sight of it made the back of Adam's throat tighten. Neither man made mention of the handkerchief as they exchanged good mornings.

Light glowed through the muslin tarp fastened over the window. The clop of hooves and the scrape of wheels prompted Adam to lift a corner and peek out. The stage had pulled up to the saloon. He considered the blood on Cook's handkerchief. "I think I better stay here. You don't need me to go to Rawlins."

Cook grasped the edge of the desk and rose from his chair, unfolding himself in painful increments. He snatched the handkerchief and stuffed it into a trouser pocket. "Don't remember changing my mind or saying you can question my orders."

Though Cook was trying to tough through his injuries, Adam knew he was not in good health or in any condition to face Carruthers or the Normans. Just because Carruthers hadn't shown up last night didn't mean he wouldn't. Adam would curse himself if he returned to Luther too late to help his friend.

But Cook wasn't giving him a choice. Adam grabbed his belongings, the Spencer, and its cartridge box and headed for the blacksmith's to collect his horse and saddle. He rode back to the saloon for coffee, breakfast, and a shave. At eight sharp, he was back on his horse, Cook's letter tucked into his vest, waiting for the passengers to board the stagecoach. They each appeared hung over. Wasn't much to do in Luther except gamble, gossip, and drink.

The driver and his messenger guard climbed into the driver's box at the front of the stage. The driver flicked the reins, and the horses jerked against their traces. The stage shuddered forward and settled into a smooth roll.

Cook watched from his office door and tipped his hat. Adam waved back and kicked his horse into a fast trot to catch the stage.

At the outskirts of town, Adam felt a stab of guilt for not confessing to Cook that he'd swapped out some of the stolen cash. But even if the sheriff knew the truth, how would that change anything concerning Carruthers and the Normans? They were coming to get the money and Francine and kill anyone who got in their way.

He looked back once more at Cook, who was now just a dark speck in the shadow along the street. Why was Cook still looking at him? And why did Adam look back? It seemed they shared a premonition they would not see each other alive again.

At the point where the road turned the bend and narrowed, Luther disappeared behind a rise of scrub and ugly rock. Adam let the stage take the lead, and he followed about fifty feet behind.

His thoughts scurried through a maze of predicaments. Once he got to Rawlins, he could say *adiós* to Luther. Let Cook deal with Carruthers and the Norman brothers. But Adam had long decided to see this problem through, so, after he delivered the report to the marshal, he'd return to Luther. Plus, he had close to ten thousand dollars stashed beneath the sheriff's office.

Couldn't leave that much money without trying a few heroics to retrieve it.

Adam kept following the stage, lulled by the rhythmic melody of hoofbeats and the crunch of iron-rimmed wheels over sand and dirt. Tobacco smoke wafted from the coach. The sun rose white hot as a ball of molten steel, and his misgivings simmered in the heat.

The hair prickled at the back of his neck. He halted the roan and sat up straight, suddenly wary, certain that someone was measuring him through rifle sights. He leaned forward, gripped the stock of his Spencer where it hung in a scabbard, and swiveled his head, squinting. Didn't see anything but brush, rocks, and dirt.

The stagecoach kept rolling away.

The tingling crept down his spine and filled his heart with foreboding. Maybe Carruthers hadn't attacked last night because he had another scheme. Adam spurred his horse into a gallop and gained on the coach, where he announced to the driver, "I'm heading back to Luther."

The driver scowled. "Why?"

"Forgot something." Adam reached into his vest and withdrew the letter. He handed it to the driver. "Make sure this gets to the marshal in Rawlins. We need his help right away."

The driver spit a mess of chew onto the trail. "All right. Watch yourself."

Adam wheeled his horse around. They'd gone maybe fifteen miles from town, so he slowed the roan to a fast trot to preserve its strength. As Adam bounced in the saddle, his thoughts percolated with dread. When he recognized the hills surrounding Luther, he urged the horse into a breakneck gallop.

He bolted around the corner where the trail widened into a road. The little town lay ahead in the dusty openness, a forlorn collection of weather-beaten buildings baking in the mid-afternoon sun. He raced through the main street and pulled up short in front of the sheriff's office, then paused a moment to catch his breath. Everything seemed peaceful, normal, dull. Francine's pony was gone, but Cook had probably taken it to the blacksmith's stable.

The drumming of his heart softened. Maybe . . . hopefully . . . he had worried himself for nothing.

He slid off his horse, whipped its reins around a post, and barged into Cook's office.

Halted at the threshold.

Cook's chair was empty. The safe was open, also empty.

Adam dashed into the jail. The cell was empty.

Francine was gone. The money was gone. Cook was gone.

Chapter Twelve

Adam feared the worst for his friend Sheriff Cook, and the knot in his guts burned like he'd swallowed poison.

He prayed to be wrong. He prayed the paranoia that had swept over him earlier, when he was certain he was being watched, was unwarranted.

But the clues in the sheriff's office confirmed his fears. The open safe reminded him of a mouth frozen in mid-gape horror. The Winchester was missing from the rifle rack. Either Cook took it or Jesse Norman had come back for his prized gun.

Francine's boots were still in the cell, under the bunk, dirty socks balled inside. Her blanket lay strewn across the floor like she'd been yanked out of the cell. Adam checked the back door to the office and found it closed, but unbarred. That could mean someone had closed the door from the outside. Or that Cook forgot to set the bar.

Right hand resting on the butt of his revolver, Adam pushed the back door open. It squeaked on its newly replaced hinges and yawned wide. He scanned the middle distance between the distant hills and the empty lot behind the office. Nothing stirred in the brush. He lowered his gaze to the dirt just outside the door and squinted at the tracks. He made out three sets of boot prints and a set of footprints, the distinct toes and soles of small bare feet. Most certainly Francine's.

Farther out from the door, another pair of boots had shuffled through the dust. Adam guessed two men had come through the front and surprised the sheriff. With his bad ear, coupled with the injuries from the gunpowder blast, Cook must not have heard the intruders. Then Francine had been hauled out of the cell, the saddlebags and fake money retrieved, and Cook and the woman were no doubt prodded at gunpoint out the door where a third outlaw waited.

He followed the prints around clumps of rabbitbrush and sage to where they met up with hoofprints behind a line of tall junipers and disappeared. The outlaws, Cook, and Francine must've mounted up—Adam counted the hoofprints—on five horses.

Tucked behind the junipers, the horses and riders would've been hidden from view. He suppressed an unwelcome admiration for the kidnapping. He and Cook had been convinced that if Carruthers and his men returned to Luther, they'd do it the same way as the last time—in the middle of the night, guns blazing. The same way Jesse had brazenly walked into the saloon and gunned down the Wests. Instead, the outlaws had snuck in like weasels, taken their prizes, and vanished.

And what if Cook himself was one of the weasels? Adam didn't like that thought, but that didn't mean it couldn't be true. If Adam had double-crossed Cook by hiding the money, then why was it so hard to believe his friend was up to the same game? Maybe Cook had cut a deal with Carruthers and skipped out with the money. Adam frowned. Then why take the girl? To keep her quiet? To punish her? And if she was also in on the swindle, why did she leave without her boots?

All these questions settled into his stomach like a helping of rancid meat.

Adam kept braiding the ideas in his head, but they always unraveled to the same conclusion—that Carruthers and his gang had kidnapped Cook and Francine. The girl had stolen the money, so it was unlikely the outlaws would forgive her.

And Jesse wouldn't forget the beating Cook had given him.

But why kidnap him? Once they'd gotten the money, why didn't they lock him in a cell, or, God forbid, if they wanted revenge, why didn't they just kill him? Maybe they were afraid someone would find his body too soon, so they meant to lead him away from town before exacting their vengeance.

He felt sick but tamped it down. If the outlaws wanted to put as much time and distance as possible between themselves and Luther, they'd have to stick to one of the two main trails. The way north to Rawlins? But that was the stagecoach route, and Adam would've run into them.

Then west. Toward Bitter Creek and Hodges Summit.

Adam strode back through the sheriff's office and then hurried to the saloon in search of a witness. Unfortunately, nobody had seen anything. He hustled from shop to shop. Again, nothing.

He visited Rex's blacksmith shop next. Francine's pony had been taken from the sheriff's office, but Cook's horse was still in Rex's stable.

The blacksmith was in his shed, crouched beside the furnace and stoking its flames with hand bellows. He turned toward Adam, quirked his eyes in surprise, and stood. A stained leather apron draped Rex's front. His gaze ranged over Adam's face, and his eyebrows cinched in distress. Without speaking, the big, bearded man strode to Adam. "There's a problem." It wasn't a question.

Adam explained what had happened. "I'm afraid they took him. God knows what'll happen, to Sheriff Cook and that girl."

Rex cussed under his breath. "I wish to heaven I'd seen something, or heard something. I don't recall anybody suspicious hanging around, or any commotion." He wiped his hands on his apron. "What are you going to do?"

"Head after Carruthers, what else?"

Rex gazed north up the street and then south. "What direction did they go?"

"I'm guessing west."

Rex's grim expression darkened. "Good luck. You'll need it."

Adam gave a nod and started back toward the sheriff's office. He halted on the sidewalk across the street from it, frustration and guilt like vinegar in his mouth. He blamed himself for Cook's grim prospects, convinced Fate was punishing him for swapping worthless paper for ten thousand of the stolen cash.

Adam's roan stood beside the hitching rack and flicked its tail. A breeze whisked dust off the hard-packed road and rippled the muslin sheet in the office window. Wind whistled through the cracks in Luther's ramshackle buildings, a soft moan that raised the hair on Adam's arms and the back of his neck.

He knew how vengeful men could shed their skins and turn into monsters, worse than anything in the Bible. He forced the ugly, ghastly thoughts out of his head.

The minutes ticked past as he steeled himself for what he had to do. Stepping into the street, he peered over his shoulder and measured the sun's height above the saloon. He had maybe five hours before dusk.

His roan was still lathered up from the hard ride back to Luther. He led his horse behind the office to let it drink its fill from the trough and chew on hay in the crib. While the horse ate and rested, he gathered supplies: coffee, hardtack, sausage, a sleeve of oatmeal crackers, extra clothes, and a spyglass. With luck, he might catch the outlaws by nightfall. But he knew it was best to plan for a few days just in case.

Adam glanced at the floorboards and wondered if he should recover the money. Use it to buy Cook's freedom if it came to that. Then he dismissed the thought. Carruthers would only double-cross him. The cash was safest here. Besides, it was never Adam's habit to give away money.

He topped off his canteens and secured the provisions in the bedroll lashed behind his saddle, then mounted up and rode back to Rex's shop. A small crowd had gathered there, likely drawn by rumors that Cook and Francine had been kidnapped. *Now* they paid attention.

The blacksmith waited outside his shed, goose gun in hand, sweat glistening on his brow and trickling into his beard. "Might be a good idea to organize a posse."

"Don't have the time. If anyone wants to help, the best thing is to stay here and keep the peace. You might get a visit from the marshal in Rawlins . . . Cook wrote him about our trouble here. If he and his deputies come looking for the sheriff, you're him until we come back."

"We?"

"Cook and me. He'll be fine." Adam wished he could believe his own words.

Rex snorted in bemusement. "Lord willing, I hope you're right. Don't you worry; I'll take care of things until you return." If he bore any resentment about taking on new responsibilities, he didn't show it.

Adam unfastened his deputy's star and bent down from his saddle, offering the badge to Rex. The blacksmith palmed the star reluctantly.

Adam squinted at the sun, hanging low over the town. "Burning daylight."

Rex stepped back and waved. "Best get going."

Adam gave the roan a light tap of his spurs, and it trotted forward. He tamped down the urge to race after Carruthers and narrow the head start, knowing both he and his horse had to pace themselves.

He rode back behind the sheriff's office and followed the hoofprints where they skirted around Luther, heading west. The path wound between shallow hills and around the junipers and brush. Just as Adam had guessed, the tracks proceeded onto the main trail to Bitter Creek, where they met up with more sets of tracks.

He examined the new hoofprints. Eight horses, if he counted right. The five in the original group: Cook, Francine, and their three kidnappers. Plus three new riders. The day before yesterday, Carruthers had ridden into town with four men. They had freed Jesse, so that made a total of six outlaws. Not good odds.

Adam urged his horse down the trail and tapped the Spencer repeater where it hung in the scabbard. He had plenty of ammo for a gunfight, but there was only one of him versus the six in Carruthers's gang. Adam had to concentrate on saving Sheriff Cook. The woman too, if possible, but he couldn't afford to worry about her. What happened to Francine was payback for saddling up with those outlaws in the first place.

Thoughts pinged in Adam's mind like buckshot. He had to focus, pay attention to the hoofprints. Otherwise, he might lose the trail or, worse, blunder into an ambush.

He followed the prints to where the road forked due west and northwest. If it were him doing the running, he'd head west toward the wild country around Hodges Summit. But the prints and recent horse dumplings continued on the fork that turned northwest over the Sweetwater Mountains and down the basin to the Rattlesnake Hills.

He still couldn't figure out why the gang had taken Cook and the woman. If Carruthers wanted simple revenge, he would've shot them both, or slit their throats, and dumped their bodies in a gully. But the prints didn't stray from the trail, and Adam never saw blood or other evidence that anyone had dismounted.

The sun settled behind the trees, and a long shadow darkened his path. Minute by minute, the landscape turned muted and gray. The air felt heavier, and the hills echoed with the harsh cawing of crows.

Adams drove his horse in a fast trot. Stars poked through the veil of the gathering dusk, and the sliver of a moon peeked above the tree line. An owl hooted. He figured to drive himself ragged until he found Cook but reconsidered that when his horse stumbled on the murky trail. The obedient roan would continue until it dropped from fatigue. But if the horse fell, it might go lame, and, if that happened, Adam couldn't hope to catch Carruthers. Better to continue the chase tomorrow at first light. He pulled the reins and halted the roan. Steam rose from its head and neck. He'd ridden the horse hard, and it needed to cool down.

The trail curved up and through a gap between two rocky bluffs. Adam could just see over the crest. An outcropping to his left would let him survey the river basin all the way to the Rattlesnake Hills.

He slid off the roan and led it up the rise. His shoulders clenched from the chill. After tying the horse to a log, he took a swig of water and slipped into his woolen coat. Then he picked his way up the outcropping. At the top, he lay on the rock and peered through the spyglass. The narrow Sweetwater River sparkled in the moonlight like a discarded necklace. He studied the inky darkness and made out the soft rounded humps of the Rattlesnake Hills beyond the river. A campfire burned in the murky distance, miles away on the southern edge of the hills.

Adam stared at the fire, a flickering yellow dot that he held steady in the lens of the spyglass. Had to be Carruthers. With Cook. Within sight, and yet might as well be on the moon.

Chapter Thirteen

"Wake up!"

Hot coffee splashed Sheriff Cook's face. He winced. The warm liquid dripped from his mustache and chin. His dry mouth tasted bitter, of something hard and thin jammed between his teeth. A stick. To muzzle him.

As he came to more fully, he realized he was curled on his side. He ached all over. His shoulders from having his arms wrenched back. His wrists and ankles from their rope bindings. His legs and feet from cramps. His face from where he'd been punched.

Cook cracked open his bruised eyelids.

Brandon Carruthers was crouching in front of him. A growth of silver beard grizzled the outlaw's oval-shaped, creased face. Thick eyebrows hooded his wrinkled, scheming eyes. Wiry silver hair had been scissored close to his scalp, and a weather-beaten slouch hat sat back on his head. Despite being called the Silver Fox, Carruthers was short and stocky, more badger than fox, a hundred and sixty pounds of pure mean.

Cook chewed at the stick tied across his mouth. His tongue felt as desiccated as leather left out to rot in the sun.

The slumber had been a respite from his agonizing delirium. His mind slipped back to yesterday morning, when he'd been at his desk, feeling smug and secure, his biggest worry the lingering pain in his ear. Then Jesse Norman was in front of him, like he'd been conjured by magic. Jesse smacked him in the face with a revolver. After that, the memories were jumbled and fragmented, like images in a broken kaleidoscope.

As best he could recollect, Jesse and another outlaw—Morgan, a redheaded ape of a man—had beaten him until he opened the safe. Jesse and Morgan took the saddlebags, then hauled Francine out of her cell. Jesse's stepbrother, Hildon, waited behind the office. Cook and Francine were put on horses and rode behind the Normans until they met with Carruthers and the rest of the gang.

Smoke from the crackling campfire brought Cook's thoughts back to the ugly here and now. His eyes roved about the camp. Bleary-eyed outlaws moved stiffly as they gathered their belongings. Carruthers turned his back on Cook and helped himself to another cup from a battered coffee pot.

On the other side of the campfire, Francine was slumped in a rag-doll heap, grimy, black hair hiding her face, her skin pink from the cold, covered in yellow and purple bruises, and striped with whip marks. The previous night, after the outlaws made camp, they passed around a bottle of whiskey, tied a rope around her neck, stripped her naked and—with the exception of Carruthers—took turns raping her by the light of the campfire, bellowing and grunting, more beasts than men. Hildon had lashed her with a whip. The stick across Cook's mouth trapped his curses and pleas for mercy. He could do nothing but avert his eyes and pray for salvation that had yet to arrive.

After the outlaws had spent themselves, Jesse led Francine by the tether while Morgan prodded her butt and legs with the smoldering end of a stick from the campfire. The tortured woman hopped and danced, hands bound behind her back, her cries smothered by the gag in her mouth. Shining eyes appeared in the gloom, from coyotes prowling close, drawn by the mayhem and the tormented sobs of wounded prey. The men drank and laughed at Francine's humiliation and misery until she collapsed at Jesse's feet. Not even poking her with the burning stick could make her react. The men grew quiet, and talked and chortled in low voices. Cook surrendered to woe and exhaustion and fell asleep.

Now he was fully awake in this living hell. The Wyoming chill clawed into him. He felt queasy with hunger. Soon after his capture, Morgan had taken his boots, so if Cook slipped off his horse—by accident or on purpose—he couldn't run far. This morning's cold torqued his toes like pincers.

Francine twitched where she lay. She was alive, but Cook doubted that was good news for her.

Hildon and the Mexican outlaw with the out-sized mustache—Adam Sanchez had called him Bigotes—readied their horses. The saddlebags with the stolen cash hung from Hildon's mount. Cook stared at the saddlebags and damned himself for how his deal with the dead West brothers had blighted his life.

Jesse walked up behind Cook, cut loose his ankle ties, and hauled him upright. Shards of pain lacerated Cook's wounded feet. He hobbled behind Jesse, crippled with suffering.

Carruthers led them from the camp to a stout oak on the other side of the clearing. Morgan straddled a thick branch high in the tree. He let go a rope, and it unfurled to reveal a simple noose tied on one end. He dropped the other end, and Bigotes caught it. Morgan dropped another rope, and Bigotes caught that one, too.

Two ropes. One for Cook, and one for Francine.

Long ago, Cook had wondered how men could calmly accept their execution. He'd seen men walk peaceably to the gallows or stand patiently before a firing squad, surrendering to their fate like a deer when a mountain lion clamped onto its neck. They'd give up and wait for the end. Why not fight until the blood stopped pumping?

Now it was Cook's turn to face his extermination. His arms

were slack, his legs barely strong enough to keep him upright. There was no peace in him, no soothing calm, just a growing numbness and a weary capitulation to the inevitable.

Jesse left Cook and returned to the camp. Carruthers lit a cigar and puffed at it, relaxed. Cook listened to the trill of sparrows and meadowlarks. Shivering, he sniffed the cigar and campfire smoke and clutched at the memories of happier days on the trail. He thought of Adam, gone to Rawlins with the stagecoach. Cook had long ago given up hope that his friend might've disobeyed orders and would find and rescue him.

A horse clopped behind Cook. Francine, still naked, sat slumped in the saddle of her pony. Her eyes were closed, her hands tied behind her back, the gag still in place. Jesse led Francine and the pony past Cook to where Carruthers stood beneath the oak tree.

Bruises, lacerations, and raw burns marred Francine's slender back and legs. When she brushed against the noose, Jesse reached up to grip her arm and bent her forward so he could loop the rope over her head. He jerked the noose snug around her neck. Even then, she didn't react. Bigotes pulled the slack out, tugging the rope until Francine sat straight with her head twisted upward. Her eyelids fluttered but remained closed. Bigotes tied the loose end of the rope to an exposed root.

Jesse faced Carruthers. "Not too late to sell her to the Cheyenne."

Carruthers shook his head. "She could still talk."

Bigotes said, "Not if we cut out her tongue."

Carruthers gave his head another shake. "If she's dead, what she knows goes with her."

"As you wish." Jesse cocked his arm and swatted the pony's rump. "See you in hell, you treacherous whore."

The pony startled forward. Francine was whisked off the saddle, and she swung free. The noose seized tight. Her eyes popped open, and her face flushed bright red. She flailed and jerked, her naked legs scissoring and pumping. Sputtering and choking, she chewed on the gag.

Moment by moment, her legs went limp. Her eyes rolled back in their sockets, and her face darkened to a gruesome shade of purple. Her bowels released, and brown filth oozed down her thighs. It dripped from her toes and spattered in the dirt. She twisted and swayed beneath the oak like the tattered flag of a beaten army.

"She dead?" Jesse asked.

Carruthers replied, "Whaddaya think?"

Jesse shrugged. "Dunno. Just asking. I've heard of folks surviving their hanging."

Bigotes drew his revolver, aimed, and fired one bullet into Francine's stomach. Blood gushed from the wound, ran down her belly, and matted her pubic hair. He holstered the pistol and declared, "If she's not dead, she's gonna be soon."

Hildon brought Cook's horse to the oak. Carruthers said, "Your turn, Sheriff."

Cook was too numb to fight. His thoughts retreated into a hole deep in his mind, and he tried to sever all feelings.

Jesse and Hildon hoisted him onto his horse. His legs went rigid, like planks of wood held together with rusty hinges. His bare feet draped outside the stirrups. Jesse grasped the horse's bit. Hildon yanked Cook forward by the shoulder and worked the noose around his neck. The noose was pulled snug, and Cook felt as if Death's hand had seized his throat.

Puffing on the cigar, Carruthers walked close. He tapped Cook's badge that hung from the sheriff's vest. "Lot of good this does, Mr. Lawman." He blew smoke into his captive's face. "So the world knows who did this to you." Carruthers reached into his coat pocket and fished out a slip of paper and the stump of a wooden pencil. He pressed the paper against the saddle, mouthed words as he scribbled them, then folded the paper and pushed it into a pocket of Cook's vest. "Should've minded your own business, Sheriff. You had your chance."

Carruthers took a step back. The rope was cinched tighter. The rough braid rasped Cook's throat. Another yank on the rope, and it dug under his jaw.

"No one is sure of their final end till it happens. This is yours." Carruthers nodded at Jesse. The big man spanked the horse, and it bolted from under Cook.

His butt bumped over the saddle, slid over the horse's haunches, and he swung free for an instant.

Then he snapped against the rope, and the noose bit his neck. His larynx collapsed into a knot of cartilage. His lungs screamed for air. Pain jolted his spine and blasted electric sparks to the ends of his fingers and toes. Blood hammered his temples, and red spilled across his vision. He kicked his legs and struggled to free his hands. His mind sprang fully alert, clawing for life and deliverance.

He twisted beneath the oak branch, spinning, the outlaws and the horses and trees and rocks blurring together. An intense cold snaked up his legs and corkscrewed through his belly. The cold slithered into his chest and coiled about his heart.

Darkness closed around him. The chill ebbed into an overwhelming sadness. From far away, he heard voices. Carruthers and his band of serpents taunting him as he died, or was it a chorus of angels welcoming him?

All went black.

A warm liquid wet his pants.

He heard a bang, and something hard and hot slammed into his guts.

He felt himself pulling away, shrinking, withering to a tiny point, until all that was left of Sheriff Nelson Cook faded to nothing.

Chapter Fourteen

Adam Sanchez rode his horse through a ford across the Sweetwater River. Water lapped the roan's shins and sprayed against Adam's boots.

The cold morning air raised goose bumps across the back of his neck. He could've used the comforting jolt of hot coffee, but, once up this morning, there wasn't time to light a fire and brew a pot. Breakfast had been a hunk of sausage and a handful of oatmeal crackers, washed down with a slug of canteen water. He rubbed the back of his gloved hand across the stubble of an unshaven jaw.

He imagined Cook lying in the dirt, blood welling from holes all over his body, paralyzed with pain, blinking at the sky and wondering why his life had come to such a gruesome end. Every minute Adam delayed meant another minute his friend crept closer to death. But Adam couldn't recklessly gallop forward or he'd find himself bleeding and dying beside Cook.

Meadowlarks and sparrows chirped in the brightening twilight, a cheery chorus to his grim temper. Head down, he chose a path across the slick river rocks, and his horse proceeded in small, searching steps.

A gunshot rang out. The birds fell silent.

Adam sat straight and reached for his revolver. His nerves zinged in alarm, and he fought to keep them under control as his gaze ricocheted across the landscape. The roan swung its head up and snorted, ears twitching, searching.

The gunshot echo faded. The report had come from ahead, the north side of the river, but, from where exactly, Adam couldn't tell.

Last night, he had placed the outlaws' campfire maybe a half mile north of the river, on a slope visible from his position on the bluff. Now that he was below the rise and looking upward, all he could see were shrubs, cottonwood, and pine clotting the wide slant of rocky ground.

His thoughts tossed in all directions. It could've been someone shooting a critter for breakfast or the careless discharge of a firearm. But his mind narrowed to the most obvious explanation. His friend Sheriff Cook was in bad trouble.

Carefully, Adam guided his horse to the riverbank. Once its hooves dug into firm sand, the roan bolted forward, and Adam slapped the reins, guiding the horse to the right. Clear of the water, he halted the roan and kept still. Gradually, the birds recommenced their singing. The dawn's light raked orange across the tops of the pines, promising warmth to chase away the morning chill.

He scanned the ground for hoofprints. This ford had been directly between the turnoff from the Bitter Creek trail and the campfire. Eight horses moving fast would've torn up the ground. Overturned rocks. Trampled grass. He wandered back and forth along the riverbank until he caught sight of the prints—upriver from his crossing by a hundred feet—a confusion of upside-down *U*'s stepping over each other and leading around the side of the hill ahead of him.

His nerves twitched, and he took a gulp from his canteen to settle them. Following the trail wasn't much of a challenge. The trick was getting the drop on these killers. If Carruthers and the Norman brothers had a sharpshooter watching the trail, Adam might wander right into a bullet. He unsheathed the Spencer from its scabbard and set the butt against his hip.

If Adam had a companion, they could take turns leapfrogging forward, each covering the other. But he was alone and had no choice. He led his horse, creeping from cover to cover. Study the terrain. Keep track of the prints. Advance a few feet to new cover. Study some more. Meanwhile, his friend might be dying.

Another gunshot echoed, a sudden bang that rolled and waned into the distance. Another blanket of silence fell across the birds. This gunshot had definitely come from up ahead, in the direction of travel.

He cocked the Spencer's hammer and tucked the rifle under his right arm. The trail of hoofprints funneled into a single file ascending a draw at his right. He gave the roan a tap of his boot heels, and the horse slipped through a stand of aspens.

He guided the roan on a course parallel to the draw, figuring Carruthers and his gang had turned west from the draw to make camp, and he'd cross their path. At every blind of cover, Adam surveyed the landscape with the Spencer close to his shoulder. Once certain he hadn't been spotted, he resumed his advance.

The sun broke over the trees and doused Adam with a burst of light and heat. The inside of his coat began to prickle. Realizing he faced a day of relentless swelter, he already missed the morning's fleeting coolness.

He advanced slowly until he sniffed wood smoke. He pushed into his stirrups and leaned back. The roan obediently halted. Adam searched the landscape for danger, and he nudged his horse into the protective shadow beside a juniper.

He inhaled the smoke and measured the smell. He imagined the smoke as Carruthers's fetid breath, and that the gang was all around him, guns drawn, holding back their laughs, waiting for the signal to blast him out of the saddle.

Nerves made his heart beat faster. If Carruthers and his men were close, Adam should've heard something. The clatter of a tin cup. The creak of leather tack. A horse's nicker. The rough chatter of coarse men.

Instead, nothing.

He doubted such a collection of men and horses could've kept quiet this long. So the gang must've broken camp.

Then why the two gunshots? Maybe, hopefully, they had been shooting game.

Adam slipped off his saddle, moving cautiously so the loudest sound he made was his boots scraping the dirt. He looped his horse's reins around the branch of a fallen log, shrugged off his coat, and draped it over the saddle. With the carbine at the ready, hunched low, he climbed up the rocks.

He stopped when he spied the campsite, a flat dirt clearing. Faint smoke ribboned from a circle of rocks in the center. Adam kept his head down behind the weeds and studied the vicinity. Seeing no one, he rose for a better look, confirmed the area was vacant, and warily entered the clearing.

Ragged patterns of moist dirt and the stench of piss marked where man and beast had relived themselves. Judging by the way the urine had soaked into the ground, Carruthers and his men had been gone at least an hour. Adam spotted a pair of knotted leather laces and crouched to examine them. They looked about the size to bind a man's wrists or ankles.

Cook's for sure. Why had they cut him loose?

Adam studied the campfire. Fragments of a broken liquor bottle lay scattered among the rocks. What smoldered surprised him: tattered clothing discarded on the dying embers. Francine's blouse. Her vest. Trousers. Undergarments.

His first thought was that she had switched sides and changed clothes. Maybe she was the reason Cook got taken by surprise. He couldn't make himself believe it, though. *She stole from them. And those gunshots . . .*

Fighting the fear that spiked in him, Adam straightened and

squared his shoulders. Carruthers and his gang shouldn't be hard to follow. Eight men on horses didn't move as efficiently as one, and dragging Cook and Francine along would slow them further.

Motion registered in the corner of his eye. Adam turned his head, thinking he might have caught the blur of a large bird winging through the trees.

Not a bird. Something swaying.

Hands tight on the carbine, Adam ducked his head for a better look through the branches. His gaze froze, and his mind stuttered as it fought against the truth of what he saw.

Sheriff Cook. Hanging on a rope. His neck distended and distorted.

Finger coiled on the carbine's trigger, Adam advanced to the oak tree. Flies clouded the air near the body. No . . . bodies.

Cook dangled from a stout branch. Francine hung from another. She appeared obscene and violated, not only because she was naked, but because her discolored and swollen flesh testified to her final moments of torment. Crusted blood surrounded the hole in her belly, and the leaked issue had dried along the contours between her legs.

Cook's corpse twisted to and fro in an abbreviated arc. The whites of his eyes were gray as the ash in the campfire. His arms were drawn and tied behind him, his hands and bare feet as swollen and purple as the tongue protruding from between his blackened lips. A dark stain had seeped across his vest, waistband, and down one trouser leg. Narrow circles of fouled earth traced the pendulum tracks beneath both bodies.

Cold fingers climbed Adam's spine, vertebra by vertebra, until the icy claws slid beneath his scalp and clamped onto his skull. He'd seen death plenty of times but seldom this gruesome. He'd known it would be bad when he set out to rescue Cook but had never once thought he'd find his friend strung up like the carcass of a hunted varmint.

Revulsion and fury made his shoulders lock in a painful cramp. If he started right off, he might catch Carruthers's gang by noon. But he couldn't leave Cook and Francine for the birds to peck until the maggot-bloated bodies burst apart. No telling when anyone would chance upon the remains and give them a decent burial.

Adam stepped to where the ropes were tied around the oak and propped the Spencer against its trunk. He unsheathed his hunting knife and sawed the blade across the rope holding Cook until the last strands tore. The rope snapped apart and scraped where it hung over the branch. Cook's body collapsed on the ground. Adam cut Francine's rope, and her corpse toppled beside the sheriff's.

Without a shovel, the best Adam could do was entomb the corpses beneath large rocks. He cut the laces binding Cook's wrists and stretched him flat on the ground where he had fallen. Thankfully, rigor mortis hadn't yet set in.

Cook's badge glinted in the sun, a seemingly useless symbol of authority considering he had died at the hands of wicked criminals. When Adam bent over to undo its pin, he spied a scrap of paper in the sheriff's vest pocket. He withdrew the paper and unfolded it. The penciled scribbling on it said:

I did this by my hand to defile the memory of this wretch Nelson Cook.
> The Silver Fox (Brandon Carruthers)

Tears stung Adam's eyes. He clenched his teeth and willed himself not to cry. He gulped hard, painfully so. The trees and the mountains seemed to melt away, and he stood alone in a vast, bleak desert of grief and remorse.

Slowly, the earth coalesced again around him. Birds chirped. Flies buzzed in his ears. A breeze moaned through the trees. His pulse thrummed with the realization that he was only holding back from a grisly chore that had to be done, and that he had to pay homage to a friend he'd cheated and let down.

He dragged Francine over and laid her alongside Cook, close together as husband and wife, or a john and his whore. Adam collected rocks big as watermelons and piled them on the bodies. The task helped him endure the hammer blows of sorrow and guilt pounding his heart.

The sun lashed him with hot, merciless rays. Perspiration drenched his back and armpits. Thirst parched his throat, but he stopped only long enough to remove his sweat-soaked shirt and hang it from a branch. His shadow shrunk beneath him, and it wasn't until late in the morning that he finished the crypt. He fetched his shirt and the carbine and paused to critique his somber handiwork. This improvised tomb might keep out coyotes and wolves, buzzards and ravens, but a bear wouldn't have a problem scattering the rocks. And the flies and worms wouldn't be stopped. Still, he'd owed it to Cook to protect the man's body best he could.

Religion never suited Adam, and he wondered what to say, what words wouldn't sound pathetic and trite against the grotesque reality of this double murder. The burnt odor of the campfire drew his attention, and the smell took him back to the war when palls of smoke unfolded like funeral shrouds over blasted dugouts and heaps of dead soldiers. As the conflict ebbed, he had witnessed generals and colonels, who spoke in high and mighty tones of temperance and honor, then ordered their troops to loot and burn the houses of the vanquished Southerners. Widows and children huddled in pathetic clusters, silhouetted by the flames devouring their homes and dignity.

So much bloodshed and misery and yet the mayhem continued.

Adam pinned Cook's sheriff badge to his own vest and

promised the mayhem would continue until it brought Carruthers and his clutch of murderers to justice.

Chapter Fifteen

Adam followed the trail left by Carruthers and his gang. The path wasn't hard to track, plenty of fresh hoofprints, disturbed rocks, and torn, flattened grass. The men had ridden their horses hard as they rushed over the uneven terrain.

Adam spurred his roan along the hill, certain he'd reach Carruthers before mid-afternoon or sooner. The challenge was to catch him unseen. Surprise wouldn't last more than a few seconds, and Adam knew the outlaws wouldn't hold still for him to collar them like they were hungover drunks.

His thoughts flipped between keeping a tight focus on his surroundings and the disturbing image of his hanged friend. Everyone died sooner or later, and mostly in circumstances lacking dignity and contentment. To lie on a comfortable bed and pass away unexpectedly in your sleep was about the only humane way to go. Trouble was, Adam didn't know of anyone who went to the big unknown so peaceably. In his line of work, men died scratching onto life while blood oozed out of their broken bodies. Or they perished from vile infection or disease. Even so, Cook didn't have to die like he did.

Adam used the barrel of his Spencer to part a tangle of vines draped over the trail. He stopped when he noticed droplets of milky sap on the leaves. The fresh liquid seeping from the vines meant they had been ripped only minutes ago.

His horse twitched, and he stroked its neck to keep it calm. Sitting tall in the saddle, he let his ears sift through the quiet.

Sparrows twittered softly in the distance. A breeze rustled the leaves.

A horse nickered.

Adam squinted as he listened for voices and the jangle of loose gear. Nothing. But that other horse was close.

Carefully, stealthily, Adam urged his roan past the vines to a curve in the trail. The edges of the hoofprints in the soft dirt were as sharp as those of newly minted coins. He halted where he could peer down the gentle slope of the hill through a gap in the brush. The gap revealed a wide, flat basin with a dry creek bed meandering down the middle. Stands of sage and sedge dotted the rocky, grassy earth, making random clumps that resembled tufts shed from a dog's winter coat.

The distance across the basin to the tree line at the far side was several hundred yards. Carruthers and his gang might have spread out, and the man riding point might well be at those trees. Adam studied the heathered browns and greens zigzagging across the ground, knowing that, at this range, a horse and rider that far away would be the size of a fly.

His best odds were to catch the outlaws grouped together and unaware. Better to hang back and keep shadowing them until they made camp.

He waited. Saw nothing. Heard nothing.

Thinking Carruthers had already crossed the creek bed and made it to the distant tree line, Adam drove his horse down the slope. Once in the basin, he was surprised to discover the shrubs and grasses were taller than expected, the bushes reaching above his head and the fescue to the withers of his roan. The trail snaked around tight corners in the dense foliage, becoming a labyrinth of narrow, twisting corridors.

A man's voice floated through the thicket. Clear and distinct. Close. Adam lowered his head and quietly cocked the hammer of his carbine.

Another man answered. "We'll rest in Casper."

Adam recognized that voice. Jesse Norman. He was on the other side of the brush.

Adam looped a finger over the trigger. His nerves sizzled like the lit fuse of a rocket.

He didn't hear anyone else, so he guessed these two were the last in line. Jesse rode trail and most certainly packed the big Winchester. If Adam took Jesse down, he could get that rifle and its valuable firepower.

The problem was, Adam was too close to them. He couldn't move forward or back away without making noise.

A horse tramped over the dirt, approaching from his right. A shadow scrolled against the wall of leaves, the ragged silhouette of a man on horseback. A bearded face appeared in a tunnel through the brush.

Jesse.

The outlaw's eyes cut to the opening. He and Adam locked gazes.

Adam poked the Spencer into the brush and pulled the trigger. Smoke blasted the leaves. He dug his boot heels into the roan's side and charged forward. Branches whipped his face and arms.

Jesse was leaning sideways in his saddle, arms thrown back, mouth open, his complexion already draining white.

Two horses walking in tandem filled the narrow trail to the left. A rider sat on the lead horse. Adam levered the Spencer and trained its muzzle on the rider, who'd sprung around in his saddle, face red with astonishment.

Adam fired. The bullet smacked the rider under the armpit. He toppled into the grass. The two horses bolted up the trail.

Adam loaded a fresh round. Jesse hung from his saddle. Blood seeped across his belly. He clutched at the saddle horn, his left leg bent over the horse, his boot tangled in its stirrup. The

Winchester lay in the weeds where he'd dropped it.

He grunted in pain, and likely in humiliation at having been caught in such an undignified pose. Slowly, his fingers worked loose, his boots slipped from the stirrups, his leg slid over the saddle, and he fell on his back amid the rocks beside the trail. His eyes pinched in disbelief and pain.

Gunfire echoed over the basin. Bullets nipped the leaves above Adam's head. Smoke from the Spencer had marked his position like a banner. Men shouted from the creek bed.

Adam had two choices: either flee and wait for another opportunity—risking Carruthers's escape—or stay and pick off the outlaws. He jammed the Spencer into its scabbard and sprang off the roan to retrieve the Winchester, then scooted to Jesse and unfastened the buckle of the big man's ammo belt.

Jesse's fists clenched and opened. His flailing, booted feet scrabbled troughs in the loose dirt. He gazed upward, straight through Adam as if Adam weren't there.

Adam tugged the ammo belt free. He pondered shooting Jesse, not to end his misery but out of spite for Jesse's part in the atrocity done to Cook and Francine. But the killer was already on the doorstep of hell, and why waste a bullet? Let him suffer.

Adam refastened the buckle and looped the belt over his shoulder, bandolier fashion. He'd shot a Winchester once before and was familiar with its action. He swung the lever just enough to see a cartridge already in the chamber.

Six men in the gang. Two down, four to go. He cocked an ear to figure out where the rest had gone. He had no illusions that he could capture them all. One, maybe two. Carruthers if possible. Adam relished seeing that maniac swing in public for all the heartache he'd caused.

A rider galloped into the middle of the creek bed, pistol drawn. A pony followed his horse, its reins tied to his saddle.

He yelled, "Jesse! Jesse!"

Adam kicked Jesse's horse and sent it sprinting up the trail. He grasped his own horse's reins and smacked them on the ground, signaling the roan to stay until called.

Hunched over, he advanced ten yards to where he could spy the rider through the brush. He sighted the Winchester on the man, who stood a hundred yards distant. It was Hildon, Jesse's stepbrother. Adam fired. The bullet grazed Hildon's leg and struck the ground in front of the horse. It reared up in panic, screaming. Hildon yanked on the reins, which panicked the pony and made it jerk its tether. The horse lost its balance and toppled onto one side, pinning the rider. It writhed and kicked, stirring up a cloud of dust. The pony struggled to pull loose, whining and kicking in alarm. The horse pushed upright, bucking and neighing.

Hildon emerged from the dust, limping for the river rocks. Adam sighted on him, but the horse and pony circled one another and blocked his shot. By the time he spotted the outlaw again, Hildon was dropping among the river rocks, out of sight.

The horse and pony nuzzled one another and quieted.

The ensuing silence was brittle as glass. Adam scanned the brush through the iron sights of the Winchester. A wide clump of brush stood twenty yards upslope from the rocks where the outlaw had fallen.

Hildon called out. Someone in the brush answered. Adam rose to a half crouch, squinted into the leaves, and looked for a target.

He did a mental tally of Carruthers's men. Two killed, one wounded. Another hidden behind the brush. That left two unaccounted for. He lowered his rifle and scanned the ragged lines of vegetation for clues to the missing outlaws' locations.

"Brandon!" Hildon cried out. "My leg's shot. Brandon!"

A shadow darkened the grass at the bottom of the brush

clump. Was it Carruthers? Adam aimed and fired. The bullet careened in a whine and a puff of dust.

"Hold up!" a man hollered from behind the shrubs. "I'm coming out."

Adam dropped back into his hide. The outlaws might be trying to draw him into the open. He pulled the Winchester tight into his shoulder. "Hildon, show yourself, too." He'd be the first to die if Carruthers pulled any stunts.

A pair of hands rose from a shallow groove in the creek bed. Then a pair of arms appeared, then a head. Hildon, all right. "Can't get up much more," he explained in a troubled, labored voice.

"Tell Carruthers no tricks or I'll drill you from here!" Adam shouted.

Leaves and grass rustled. A horse walked into the open, a rider in the saddle, hands raised. But it wasn't Carruthers.

Another horse and rider bolted from behind the brush and galloped away from Adam.

There's Carruthers.

Adam aimed and fired. The horse cocked its head back and then down. Its neck curled forward. The horse's forelegs collapsed, and its body somersaulted. Adam had missed Carruthers but hit the horse.

Carruthers let go of the reins and swung his boots from the stirrups. Tossed free, his momentum carried him tumbling across the ground. The horse rolled onto its side and lay still. At the instant Carruthers stopped sliding through the dirt, Adam fired. The bullet tore the ground near the outlaw's face. Adam levered another round and fired again, the bullet careening by Carruthers's hand. Lightning fast, Adam levered again. He shouted, "Hold still! Otherwise the next bullet has your name on it."

Carruthers propped himself on his knees and raised both

hands. Adams felt mild satisfaction. With this Winchester he was the equal of half a dozen sharpshooters. He yelled at the rider, "Hildon, come here! And, Carruthers, get on your feet and do the same."

Adam kept the Winchester trained on them as they gathered by the wounded outlaw. "Everybody toss all your guns and knives into a pile. You on the horse, dismount slowly and get on your knees, hands on your head." Still hidden in shadow, Adam kept an eye out for the sixth outlaw as he slipped cartridges from the gun belt and topped off the Winchester.

The three gang members in view heaped their guns and knives together. They knelt in a tight circle, the wounded Hildon leaning sideways to favor his bad leg.

Keeping the rifle trained on Carruthers, Adam crept from behind cover. His gaze darted from the men to the trees and brush behind them.

Hildon gulped and grimaced. A bandana had been tied around his right calf, and the lower part of his trouser leg was stained with blood. Flies buzzed around the wound. The second outlaw tracked Adam's approach with wary, condemning eyes. A hat brim kept Carruthers's face in shadow.

Adam recognized Francine's pony tethered to Hildon's horse. It still carried her saddlebags, thick with the fake money.

Adam walked close enough to Carruthers to read the evil shine in the killer's eyes. If the outlaws had learned the stolen money was mostly worthless paper, they would've said so. But they hadn't. The foolish, deadly charade continued.

The gang leader sneered, looked away, and spat. Adam kicked him in the chest. Carruthers fell back, his glare snagging Adam like his eyes had barbs.

Adam said, "Just making sure you don't get the impression I'm a gentleman. The reason I haven't killed you all is that I don't want to cheat the hangman. He deserves the work." He made sure the Winchester was pointed at Carruthers. "But push me, and he'll have to live with the disappointment."

Adam panned the rifle across the group. "You're missing a man. The one with the big mustache. Bigotes. Where is he?"

Everyone kept silent. Carruthers remained on his side, his hands inching back toward his hat.

Adam trained the rifle on Carruthers's belly. "Keep your hands where I can see them." He ordered the third man—his name was Red—to tie Carruthers's and Hildon's wrists, hands in front, with leather cord. Still no sign of Bigotes, that son of a bitch with the long mustache. Galloped off when Carruthers tried to flee, maybe. Adam tested the bonds, waited another moment or two, then set down the Winchester just long enough to tie Red's hands.

He checked the men for hidden weapons and found none. As he collected their surrendered pistols, he emptied them of cartridges and stowed the guns and knives in his saddlebags. He gathered the horses, seven total. Jesse and the other dead outlaw he likewise stripped of their pistols and knives, leaving their bodies on the trail where they had fallen.

Adam surveyed the landscape. Bigotes was nowhere in sight. Back in Luther, he'd seemed tough and vicious, not the type to turn tail and leave his crew. It appeared he had, though. Criminals like these scum had the scruples of sewer rats.

Adam rounded up his roan and returned to the trail. He untied Francine's pony and secured it to his saddle. "Everyone, mount up." He nodded toward the south. "You all know the way back to Luther. Get going."

Carruthers started for point with Jesse's horse in tow, Red rode second and tethered to the late sheriff's horse, Hildon fifth in line with another horse. Adam followed on his roan, leading Francine's pony with the bags full of fake money.

He avoided the trail they'd followed here. Too many switchbacks and places to tempt Carruthers. Better loop on a path over open ground. He hadn't figured capturing this many prisoners and their mounts. The ride to Luther was one night and a wake-up. Maybe he could drive them all night. Another worry was how to lose the fake money. Find a way to burn it. Have the saddlebags fall into a ravine. Anything to hide his part in this bloody circus.

They stuck close to the dry creek bed. In mid-afternoon, water percolated into shallow pools from the swales underneath. Adam figured they'd reach the Sweetwater River soon. Take a break. Brew coffee. Rest the horses.

Their path meandered onto flat ground between rounded masses of rocks. They had just cleared the rocks when a gunshot broke the quiet.

Adam whirled in his saddle. A boll of smoke drifted from the top of a pile of large boulders. He galloped ahead of Carruthers, putting the gang between the shooter and himself.

Carruthers gave a dirty grin. "You were asking about my sixth man, you stupid tin-horn bastard. Well, he found you."

Chapter Sixteen

Dry mouthed, nerves zinging in apprehension, Adam scanned the boulders. Everything around him stood out in bizarre relief, trees and rocks like paper cutouts and the outlaws on their horses like cardboard puppets.

Carruthers rocked in his saddle and grinned. The color returned to Hildon's cheeks, and mirth replaced the pain on his face. Cracked lips framed crooked, yellow teeth as they laughed. Adam heard nothing but the pounding of his pulse in his ears.

The smoke from the first shot had scarcely faded when a second bullet cracked past his ear, and another dust puff blossomed. Adam cringed and looked for cover. Several slabs of rock—gray, flat, and wide—stuck out from the ground like giant crooked tombstones fifty yards behind him. A ruff of shrubs and weeds around the rocks provided more concealment. He might make their safety, or the shooter might drill him. Too risky.

Hearing slowly returned to his ears: the rustle of clothing and riding tack, the pawing of hooves, air bellowing through the horses' nostrils. He yelled at the three outlaws to crowd together. He kept his head down and tucked his horse behind them.

"You're a real hero, aren't you?" Carruthers taunted. "Using us as shields."

Adam jabbed him in the back with the Winchester. "Shut your yap. You're lucky I haven't left you for the buzzards." He worked loose the tethers of the gang's extra horses but kept Francine's pony cinched to his mount. He said to Carruthers, "Now toss me your reins."

The outlaw flicked the reins toward him. Adam balled them in his left hand. His right hand held the rifle and his own reins. In this awkward arrangement, he could only manage one shot from the Winchester. He motioned to the rocks. "We're making a dash for it. Any of you hold back, and I'll shoot you."

Another bullet ricocheted behind Adam. He yanked the reins of Carruthers's horse and kept the rifle trained on Hildon and Red. He turned his horse toward the rocks, Carruthers behind on his left, Hildon and Red to the right. Adam kicked his heels into his roan's side and shouted.

The horses, already jumpy, burst into a pell-mell rush. Though the three extra horses had been freed, they gaggled alongside. Adam bounced in his saddle, his mind's eye fixed on the sharpshooter, aware of the sights aligning on his back.

His intuition screamed a warning, and he jerked his horse to the left, bumping against Carruthers. A bullet zinged past his ear like an angry hornet.

He glanced to the right. Red wore an expression like a man staring over a cliff and about to drop into the abyss. Hildon had broken away. Adam fired at him, missed, and regretted what he'd done. To reload the rifle he'd have to loosen the reins.

Carruthers's horse rammed into his. The outlaw leaned from his saddle, arms outstretched, his bound hands straining to shove Adam to the ground.

Terror spiked through him, then a rush of anger beat it back down. He clamped his legs around his horse and rammed the butt of the Winchester against Carruthers's chest, knocking him back. Adam drew enough slack in the reins to lever a fresh round into the rifle. But Hildon had disappeared.

Adam's horse ran even with the rocks, and he jerked the

reins for a quick dodge to get behind the first slab. He yanked Carruthers's horse with him. Sensing danger, the horses jostled against each other, forcing Carruthers and Red to press into Adam. He pushed them back with the Winchester and shouted, "Get off your horses!"

A bullet careened off the edge of the rock. Fragments nipped Adam's cheek and neck. He ducked, chest heaving, and wiped the blood trickling from his wounds. He watched Carruthers and Red dismount. Another shot rang out, spooking the loose horses, and off they ran. The two outlaws stood thirty feet behind the rock, in the open, staring, waiting for this trap to play out.

The next rocks lay to Adam's right, two slabs set side by side with enough room between them for his horse and the pony. He swung off his roan and pointed it toward the narrow gap. He slapped its haunches, and it trotted forward, leading the pony into cover.

A bullet whistled by his face. This round came from the distant trees at his left, far from the other shots. The sharpshooter couldn't have moved that fast. Carruthers must've had more men waiting. And now Hildon had escaped to join their ranks.

Adam pressed his back against the rock and sank low so the weeds and shrubs concealed him. As he mulled his options, he plucked a cartridge from the gun belt and topped off the Winchester. To the east, on the other side of the rock, the sharpshooter waited in his rampart among the boulders. To the south and west, the ground scrolled across shallow, grassy hills. To the north, a ragged line of scrub trees followed the trail. The last shot had come from that direction. A rifleman could scramble from tree to tree, sneaking closer while the first sharpshooter kept Adam pinned in place. Moments ago, he had been hoping for coffee and a chance to stretch his legs. Now he was trapped between closing pincers.

"What's the plan now, Sheriff?" Carruthers yelled, clearly amused. Even Red looked entertained.

The sun topped the rock, and its rays beat down on Adam like he was under a magnifying glass. Perspiration seeped from his heated skin. A growing thirst tormented his throat. A canteen hung from his saddle, but he couldn't risk fetching it. "You two stay put."

Carruthers and Red sat on the ground among the weeds.

"It's getting mighty hot." The silver-headed outlaw tilted his head to squint at the sun. "Whatever trick you got playing in your head, you better get on it before we bake like meat pies." Carruthers sounded like he was enjoying himself.

The minutes passed. The day grew more miserable. Intermittent shots snapped against the rock, warning Adam to stay down. As much as he wanted to consider more pleasant circumstances to keep his hopes buoyed, he couldn't let his mind wander. He kept listening for the scratch of leather on dirt or the creak of twigs underfoot. Carruthers and Red rested on their backs, hats covering their faces, taking a nap as this mayhem unfolded.

The sun angled midway in the afternoon sky, catching Adam in the full glare of the light and heat reflected from the gray slab. A headache drummed against the front of his skull. The best ploy he could try was to wait until dark, get on his horse, and take the pony and Carruthers with him. But the shooters had no doubt figured on that.

Adam realized they hadn't fired for a while. Maybe thirty minutes. He wanted to believe the outlaws had given up but was certain they had repositioned to flush him from cover. To test his guess, he plucked a fist-sized rock that lay near his boot and chucked it at Carruthers. The rock bounced off the outlaw's chest, and he stirred with a string of expletives.

"You and Red, wake your asses up," Adam scolded. The two men sat up. "On your feet." He threatened them with the Winchester. "Now."

Carruthers and Red rolled to their hands and knees and pushed upwards from the weeds.

A volley of shots gnawed the air. Carruthers and Red flattened themselves in the dirt. Adam glimpsed the silhouette of a head and shoulders as someone ducked behind a tree to the north, a hundred yards distant. Adam fired a quick shot and missed. The smoke from his muzzle was bait for a fusillade that chewed the rock above his head.

At least four rifles. Four gunmen hunting for him. The rate of fire slowed but remained steady, about one shot every ten seconds.

Then the rifles suddenly ripped loose. Shots came at Adam from the left and right. The outlaws must've grown impatient and decided to rush him. He hesitated, not sure if he stood a better chance dashing for his horse or staying behind cover to fight it out.

More shots and the thunder of hooves approached from the south. More outlaws for certain. Adam readied the Winchester, hoping he could drop enough of them for the rest to reconsider the attack.

The shooting grew intense. He hunkered close to the rock, but none of the bullets splattered around him. Instead, the shooters and the oncoming riders were apparently firing at each other. He slid to the side of a boulder and peeked around the corner. A dozen men galloped toward him, obscured by dust and gun smoke. A red and white pennant fluttered on a staff held by one of them. A cavalry pennant.

Adam looked to the sky and mouthed a prayer of gratitude.

The horse soldiers spread out and kept up a steady volley with their revolvers and single-shot Spencers. After a few seconds, the shooting from the outlaws stopped. One soldier ordered the party to cease fire. Another man relayed the order and instructed the others to set up a picket and secure the area.

Adam studied the soldiers. The closest two were of smaller stature than the rest. Their blue army tunics were unbuttoned, and long, braided plaits hung from under their hats. Instead of trousers and boots, they wore buckskin leggings and moccasins. Indian scouts. The other men, with the exception of the one giving orders, had dark skin in shades from coffee with milk to rich ebony. Buffalo soldiers. From the Tenth Cavalry.

Adam shouted, "Don't shoot!" He laid the Winchester by his feet and stood, hands held high.

Scowling and wary, the Indian scouts trotted closer. Four of the buffalo soldiers kept their carbines at the ready and formed a semi-circle between the rocks and where the outlaws had been. The other soldiers followed the scouts. The man in charge was white, though his skin was ruddy and peeling like an overcooked tomato. He wore the gold-embroidered shoulder straps of a lieutenant. An older buffalo soldier rode alongside. He had a thick mustache and a weather-beaten face, and his tunic bore the chevrons of a sergeant.

The soldiers rode close, taking in Adam, Carruthers, Red, and the assorted horses.

Adam tapped his sheriff's badge and introduced himself. "Adam Sanchez, acting sheriff of Luther. Much obliged for your timely and welcome intervention." He pointed to Carruthers and Red. "The fellows shooting at you are friends of these two criminals." He said nothing of the fake money in the pony's saddlebags.

The lieutenant asked, "And who are they?"

"The older one is Brandon Carruthers, the Silver Fox. The other is named Red, though I don't know much about him except that he doesn't have the sense to keep better company."

The lieutenant unbuttoned his tunic, reached in, and withdrew a sheaf of folded papers. He shuffled them, unfolded one paper, held it up, and studied Carruthers. Then he nodded in satisfaction and passed the paper to the sergeant, who compared it to Carruthers and then handed the paper to Adam.

The paper was a poster with a crude drawing of a head that sort of resembled Carruthers.

Wanted for robbery and murder.
Brandon Carruthers.
A.K.A. The Silver Fox. $1,000 Reward.

This was followed by a dense paragraph giving details of Carruthers's appearance, his manner, and more about his crimes.

Adam folded the paper and returned it to the lieutenant. "I would appreciate your assistance bringing these men to justice. I'm taking them to Luther for a fair trial and, if justice prevails, a hanging."

The lieutenant leaned close to the sergeant, and they held a whispered conversation. The lieutenant glanced at where the other shooters had been. "I imagine the comrades of these rascals will continue to harass you. We're a ways from Fort Washakie. Escorting you to Luther will make for a good excuse to bunk under a roof and get some decent food."

"It'll be on the house, I promise."

The lieutenant nodded. "Gather your prisoners and horses. Sergeant, assemble the detail."

The sergeant said something Adam didn't understand. Indian talk. The scouts collected the loose horses and brought them back.

Adam returned to his horse and drank plenty from the canteen. He pondered his next dilemma: how to get rid of the fake money once and for all. He'd been lucky so far that no one had discovered his deception. But, once he returned to Luther, he would have to reveal the contents of the saddlebags. His plan was to lose them before it was too late. He couldn't throw the bags into the brush without being seen. Once they stopped to bivouac, he doubted he could empty the money into the campfire or sneak away and burn it. Then inspiration struck. He pretended to cinch the pony's saddlebags and instead loosened the straps.

He mounted his horse, while the soldiers herded Carruthers and Red to their mounts at gunpoint. They formed a column, the lieutenant and four soldiers in the lead, then Adam and the prisoners, followed by the sergeant and the remaining soldiers. When the lieutenant gave the order to move out, the scouts scrambled ahead.

By late afternoon the column arrived at the Sweetwater River. The scouts had already picked a place to ford and waited on the other side. The sergeant divided his men into two groups, one to wade across while the others watched, carbines cradled.

Adam studied the river, turbulent with winter runoff, and the way the water splashed around the horses' legs. One of the soldiers wandered downstream, and his horse abruptly sank to its belly. The sergeant cursed at him, and the soldier guided his horse back to shallow water.

When Adam got the signal to proceed, he lingered to let Carruthers and Red cross first. Upon reaching the middle of the river, Adam moved toward the spot where the soldier had almost fallen in and made his horse bump against the pony. It stepped to the left, lost its footing, and stumbled into a wide hole. Sinking to its withers, the pony lunged toward Adam, but he maneuvered his horse in the way. The pony shrieked and thrashed in the water, splashing Adam, soaking his clothes. The soldiers yelled. One of the scouts rushed toward him.

Adam shouted, "I got it!" He reached down and grasped the pony's bridle. The pony stared at him and lunged forward.

Adam anchored his boots in the stirrups to keep from getting dragged over. He leaned against the pony's head and pushed away. The pony thrashed once more. The saddlebags worked loose. The pony lunged again, Adam pushed again, and the pony sank to its neck, legs scrambling for purchase against the edge of the hole. When the pony bucked upward, the saddlebags were gone.

Hallelujah.

Adam tugged at the bridle and led the pony to the shallow ford. The afternoon air chilled his wet clothes. A few soldiers called out, "You lost your saddlebags," but Adam acted like he didn't hear. He kept fussing with the pony until he reached the riverbank.

The lieutenant chided him. "Hope you don't mind losing the saddlebags."

Adam forced himself to suppress a laugh. Instead, he scowled. "Couldn't be helped."

"It was money," Carruthers interrupted sourly.

The lieutenant said, "We could scout along the riverbank and see where it turns up."

Adam looked at the river, but thankfully all he saw was water frothing over the rocks. "It wasn't my money. Belonged to some bank in Kansas. Its loss is their problem." He glanced at Carruthers and Red. "It's more important that I get these two killers behind bars."

Chapter Seventeen

Adam and his cavalry escort rode into Luther. Soldiers flanked Carruthers and Red, who slumped in their saddles, heads down, looking shriveled. Hildon and the remaining gang never appeared. Adam figured they should've taken this setback as a lesson to wise up and migrate to safer pastures.

Somehow, in that mysterious way rumor wafts through the air, word of the captured outlaws had reached town. The locals waited along the dusty main street to stare with curiosity and satisfaction at the procession. Barefoot boys and girls whooped and raced alongside the horses. Adam reflected on the stories he remembered of Caesar returning to Rome, victorious, the enemies of the empire in chains.

People yelled catcalls at his prisoners.

"Scoundrels!"

"Murderers!"

"Monsters!"

Carruthers replied to the taunts with a lift of his chin and a warped smile, but, when someone shouted, "We'll cheer when you swing from the gallows, you bastard," his shoulders sagged again, and his head dipped. Red trailed behind him, looking scared, more whipped dog than wanted criminal.

The town elders waited under the awning in front of the sheriff's office. A pane of new glass had replaced the boards covering the front window. They stood on the shaded sidewalk: the blacksmith, Burt Rex; the merchant, Daryl Anderson; the undertaker, Edward Blair; and the minister. Save for the reverend, all the men were armed, cradling shotguns or with revolvers stuck into their waistbands.

The soldiers formed a cordon that funneled Adam and the two prisoners to the office. Men and women shuffled closer.

The elders greeted Adam's approach with a collective nod. He acknowledged them by touching the brim of his hat and slid off his horse.

Rex limped from the sidewalk, stepping out of the shadow and into the sunlight. He switched his shotgun to his other hand and extended one of his huge, square-fingered mitts. His mustache and heavy beard framed a warm smile. "Welcome back," he said, eyes fixed on the badge pinned to Adam's lapel. "Sheriff."

Adam's heart swelled at the comment. He swept his eyes across the audience of well-wishers and absorbed their admiring gazes. Never in his life had he been the object of such public adulation. Fact was, he was often the man the authorities held in contempt. This moment should have felt so very wrong. Now he stood before the assembly, unshaven, unkempt, smelling of horse, but their hero nonetheless, regal and proud.

He turned back to Rex. "How's my new deputy?"

The blacksmith put his hand over the metal star on his shirt. "Was hoping this was temporary." His expression turned somber. "Nelson Cook? The woman?"

The reminder of their fate, especially his friend's, brought back the grief and anger. Adam shook his head. "They both suffered heinous deaths." He pointed at Carruthers and raised his voice. "By the word, if not the deed, of this man, the accused." A wave of disgust rippled through the townspeople. Adam shifted his finger. "And his accomplice."

Carruthers and Red clenched their jaws and stared into the distance.

Adam gripped Rex's thick arm. "I need you by my side on a permanent basis. We'll perform the formalities later."

The lieutenant dismounted and peeled off his gloves. Adam introduced him and then mentioned the sergeant, who remained on his horse. The sergeant saluted.

Adam climbed onto the sidewalk to better address the crowd. "If it hadn't been for the providential arrival of these valiant men in uniform, justice might have never prevailed over these two wicked scoundrels." *Listen to yourself, you're sounding like a politician.* He sought out Wald and said, "Gunter, I promised these soldiers dining and quarters in your fine establishment."

The saloon proprietor eyed the colored troopers with hesitation.

"At the county's expense of course," Adam continued. Noting the dismissive glare Wald had given the buffalo soldiers, he added sharply, "I hope that's not a problem."

"No, no," Wald replied with an oily bow. "Our brave custodians of the peace will be treated to hospitality second to none."

Adam turned to the undertaker. "Mr. Blair, I need you to assemble a party to recover the remains of our unfortunate late sheriff and Miss Francine Mills and return them to Luther for a proper burial. You and I will meet later to negotiate the details and compensation."

Blair nodded and immediately began counting the expected profit on his fingertips. "I'll draft a letter of agreement."

Adam ordered Carruthers and Red taken off their horses and led into the jail, where they were shackled to the cell bars. The lieutenant commanded his men to guard the prisoners until the locals could take over. After checking to make sure the prisoners were secure, Adam grabbed a change of clothes and headed to the Mountain View to give his grimy body a good scrubbing. Afterwards, when Lucy finished trimming him with her razor and scissors, he entered the saloon as he was accustomed: neatly combed, in crisply pressed shirt and trousers, polished boots, shiny revolvers, his shaved face tingling with cologne. He had hoped for conversation with Gloria, the merchant's wife, until Jake the saloon keep whispered that she had gone upstairs to help the lieutenant with the accommodations.

Adam sat at a table at the back of the bar and ordered a steak. Ceiling lanterns bathed the interior with a warm glow and overlapping, undulating shadows. The colored soldiers kept to themselves. Some drank coffee and picked at frosted cake, others smoked and played cards. One plucked an out-of-tune fiddle he had spotted and retrieved from behind the bar.

Adam sipped Kentucky bourbon poured from the fresh bottle on his table. The sergeant approached, his gaze flicking across the saloon in circumspect arcs, telegraphing that he had a private matter to discuss. Adam offered him a seat. One of the Indian scouts followed the sergeant but refused a chair, apparently preferring to stand. The scout wasn't much taller than a teenage white boy and was just as scrawny, but, with his weathered skin, he looked as experienced and mean as an old coyote. A Schofield revolver and a stag-handled knife were tucked into his waist sash.

"I noticed none of your men are drinking," Adam said.

"We're prohibited to do so when on patrol." The sergeant spoke like his throat remained coated with trail dust. The big man arranged his gangly frame in the chair. His dusky, mustached face looked hewn from stained mahogany.

"You're not on patrol. You're in my town."

"While we are away from the fort, we are on patrol."

"Shame, considering drinks are on the house."

"Yes, sir, it is a damn shame."

Adam corked the whiskey and pushed the bottle across the table to the sergeant. "But there is no regulation against you accepting this gift, is there? As long as you don't drink while on patrol?"

The sergeant palmed the bottle and pulled it closer. "My thirst can wait until I am back at the fort and off duty. Much obliged, Sheriff."

Jake brought Adam's steak dinner, still steaming and smelling delicious. He was famished and had held his appetite at bay just to savor this reward. Without prompting, the sergeant mentioned that he'd already eaten.

Adam carved into the succulent meat and forked a chunk between his lips. "Then what's still eating *you*, sergeant?"

The sergeant glanced back at the Indian scout, who gestured and explained in his native tongue. The sergeant translated. "Talons of the Eagle says he found the saddlebags you lost."

Adam felt his heart recoil as though he'd been kicked by a mule. Despite the morsel of moist beef on his tongue, his mouth instantly parched.

The money. *The fake money.* He was so certain his ruse had worked that he hadn't once thought of the missing "cash" since last night. Now it was back, like a rash that refused a cure. He forced himself to keep chewing and downed the meat with a dry, painful swallow. The sergeant allowed him a pull of the whiskey. Adam cut the steak again so he wouldn't have to meet the sergeant's eyes. "And you bring me this information why?"

Talons of the Eagle spoke and paused, then spoke and paused some more as the sergeant translated in a steady, muffled voice. "I'm not a learned man, but I am schooled in the ways of the world and the white man, the ones who you serve, comanchero. The men you arrested had robbed a bank and carried the money in the saddlebags of the pony tied to your horse. Someone entrusted with such a sum surely would have panicked at its loss. You seemed almost relieved."

Adam wiped his mouth and dropped the napkin beside his

plate. His dinner was getting cold, but, no matter, he had lost his appetite. "What is your scout's point, sergeant?"

Talons of the Eagle noticed Adam's distress and smiled wryly. He spoke again, and the sergeant translated. "We did find money. And paper cut to look like money. Some of it remained in the saddlebags. Some of it was scattered along the river banks and along the rocks."

"We?"

The sergeant explained. "Talons of the Eagle and He Who Whistles, the other scout."

Adam kept his face rock rigid. "That's what you think was in the bags? Money and paper?"

"Yes."

Adam wanted to clear his throat but had to hide any clue that betrayed his guilt. "Then I suppose that's the case. I never looked in the bags."

The sergeant and the Indian scout began a spirited exchange. Eventually the sergeant relented to the scout's argument and faced Adam. "We collected two hundred and fifteen dollars in government notes. Who does that money belong to?"

Adam met the scout's eyes, lustrous and piercing inside their leathery slits. "I'm going to report the stolen bank money was lost. If anyone finds random cash, I would say it belongs to them."

"It is a large amount."

"Then I'd be careful about how I spent it. You don't want the wrong people asking questions and you giving them answers they don't want to believe."

Talons of the Eagle glowered at Adam for a long moment, hardened his jaw, and flexed his sinewy arms. Who knew what crossed his scheming mind? The sergeant shifted in his chair to get out of the way. Adam's smile flattened into a narrow, suspicious line, and his right hand twitched for his holster.

The scout's swarthy, wrinkled face bunched around a ragged, toothy grin as he spoke. The sergeant translated his words with a relieved sigh. "I learn yet another lesson at the knee of you devils, white or Mexican. Your forked tongues never get tied into knots."

Talons of the Eagle patted the sergeant's shoulder and uttered some final words, which the soldier translated: "Many Yellow Stripes and I will keep this secret. Of money lost and other money found and put to good use, no questions asked."

Adam let himself relax. "Just be smart about it."

The sergeant stood, whiskey bottle in hand, and dismissed himself and the scout. The thirst for alcohol returned, and Adam ordered another bottle. He nibbled at his cooled steak and potatoes and green beans and sipped a hearty slug of 80 proof. Realizing that he had no bed of his own—other than the bench in the sheriff's office—raised the thought that he needed to celebrate dodging yet another near miss with catastrophe by enjoying the attentions of a woman. But if there was any shameless celebrating going on tonight, it was Mrs. Daryl Anderson and her guest, the army lieutenant. Adam raised his glass and offered a toast to them and her cuckolded husband.

He finished one short glass of whiskey, cleaned his plate, and treated himself to coffee and a slice of cake. Tipsy and suddenly weary, he trudged upstairs to a room and a solitary bed, compliments of the Mountain View.

The next morning he woke early, ate a quick breakfast, and went back to the office before the rooster at the end of the street quit crowing. He left the front door open to air out the place, then relieved the night guard and inspected his prisoners. The cell stank of human refuse, and flies clouded the rim of the bucket serving as a chamber pot. Carruthers lay on the bunk, boots off, one ankle chained to a cell bar. Red slept on the floor, heaped under a blanket, and was also tethered by a stout chain.

Neither man stirred. Burt Rex arrived, deputy badge askew on his woolen vest. Adam asked him to summon an armed crew to watch the prisoners rinse their bucket outside, clean up, and get them breakfast—the pretense of civility before their eventual date with justice and the hangman.

Adam took his place behind the desk and wrote out the charges against Brandon Carruthers and Red, whose given name he'd learned was Morgan Speight. Adam wasn't sure of what proper legal terms to use. A court clerk would have to figure that out. He penned a letter to the governor requesting that a judge come to Luther to convene and preside over a trial.

As he reached his quill pen toward the inkwell, he paused and reflected on what he was doing. He was amazed by how easily he had settled into these administrative duties. He had always figured himself to be a rambling man yet was strangely pleased with this new station in life.

He put the pen down and reached into his shirt pocket to retrieve the wallet with Tess's letter. He slipped the envelope from the wallet but didn't open it, as he knew its contents by heart. *A wounded heart.* Tess had spurned him because of his rootless and itinerant résumé. What would she think of him now? As a sheriff. A lawman.

Adam turned in his chair and glanced at the bookcase. It still bore the scars and scorch marks of the gunpowder explosion. Beneath the floorboards rested the sack of missing money. Close to ten thousand dollars. He felt sure the serial numbers had been documented in a ledger, so cashing in such a large sum would attract the eyes of the banking authorities. When he had the chance, he would head into Mexico with the money. Convert it into gold. Sell the gold along the way back and stash his earnings in a bank. At that point, he would possess both the appropriate office and finances to prove worthy of Tess.

But that glad thought didn't last long. Surely she had moved on. And so should he.

Adam slipped the letter back into the wallet and tucked the wallet in his pocket. And what of Cook's share, the eight thousand? Where could he have stashed it? When did he have the opportunity to hide that sum? Adam shook his head, thinking that money must be lost forever. He dipped the pen and continued his paperwork.

Someone knocked on the doorjamb. Adam glanced up and saw the lieutenant. The man looked parade ready: black hat and blue tunic dusted and blotted clean, brass gleaming, pink face smooth, mustache waxed, expression polished by a good night's rest and Mrs. Anderson's randy affections.

Adam laid the pen aside and sat back to let the papers dry. He beckoned the officer inside.

The lieutenant removed his hat. His shiny boots thumped the floor as he entered. "I need to thank you and the town for your generosity."

Adam waved him off. "Nothing of the sort. If you and your men hadn't rescued me, I'd be rotting in the wilderness along with Sheriff Cook and Miss Francine Mills."

The lieutenant clasped his hands behind his back and rocked on his heels. His gaze traveled the room. "My sergeant told me you gave him a bottle of whiskey."

"I did. In gratitude for your bravery." Adam's gut clenched. *What else did the sergeant tell you?*

The lieutenant grinned. He looked down his long, sunburned nose at Adam. "Just making sure. The troops can get a little light fingered on occasion." He donned his hat. "If there is nothing else, I must continue my patrol."

"I'd like you to stay." Adam winged a thumb toward the jail cell. "Hildon Norman is still on the loose, and he's not resting while his buddies simmer behind bars. He was brazen enough to attack this town once, and I'd be surprised if he didn't return to spring Carruthers loose."

The lieutenant shook his head. "We're Indian fighters, not marshals. We helped you as a matter of opportunity, but I couldn't post myself here without orders."

Adam nodded to mask a growing nervousness. "Where are you going?"

"Why?"

"If you're going to Laramie, I have something for you." Adam gathered the papers on his desk. He retrieved a manila envelope from a drawer, slid the papers inside, and offered the envelope. "Please deliver these to the magistrate's office. I need to start the process for a trial."

The lieutenant took the envelope. "I'll personally see that he gets them." He and Adam shook hands. "Good luck to you, Sheriff."

The sergeant waited outside on his horse. The detachment had assembled in two columns, the red and white guidon at the front and held high. The Indian scouts paced alongside on their ponies. This time of the morning, most of the locals were busy with chores, but a few watched from under the awnings.

The lieutenant climbed on his horse. Adam and the sergeant traded fleeting, knowing glances. Talons of the Eagle never looked at him.

The lieutenant gave an order to the sergeant, who repeated the command, sharply. The ten soldiers and two scouts started east out of Luther, the horseshoes of their mounts flashing iron *U*'s through the roiling dust.

Adam leaned against an awning post and watched them until they melted into the distance. He wanted to breathe easier, believe this troublesome saga was over, but a vexing anxiety told him that he and the town remained in danger.

Chapter Eighteen

Adam and his deputy Burt Rex stood on a patch of dirt between the blacksmith's shop and the back of his house. The late morning sun painted the surrounding landscape in bright colors. Laundry fluttered from a clothesline. Rex's wife peeked from around a door, face tense with worry.

The big blacksmith smelled of wood smoke and the metallic tang of iron. His shop yawned open behind him. Embers popped and spun from the furnace inside. A hammer and a long flat piece of iron lay on the anvil by the furnace. Horses whinnied in the stable.

"It's a good chance that Hildon Norman and his gang will return," Adam began. "They'll try to free Carruthers."

Rex leaned on his cane. Grimacing, he shifted uncomfortably, partly from his leg scar acting up but most likely because Adam had come by with this disquieting news. He shooed a fly from the bald spot on his scalp. "You think that's possible?"

Last night had passed without trouble, but Adam knew he couldn't get complacent. "I'd rather be wrong," he said, "but these murderers have gotten the drop on me before. Best we remain vigilant."

Rex nodded as he pondered the situation. "What about the other fellow?"

"Morgan Speight?" Adam shook his head. "I think they'd sooner let him rot in place. If they have the chance to spring him, they will. But the Silver Fox will be the object of their attention."

"Can't understand why they don't cut their losses and let us be."

"We're dealing with criminals who have their own twisted code of honor."

"The town can't afford to have men stand guard while there's work to be done."

"I understand." Adam had picked up a long stick and scratched a map of Main Street in the dirt. "Here's my plan. Since you know the folks here, you select a posse. Have them go about their business but keep their guns handy." A town the size of Luther didn't have men to spare. Only one had offered to help, and he was watching the prisoners while Adam organized this defense.

Adam pointed to one rectangle. "This is the Mountain View. If the shooting starts, and God forbid it does, I want you to make sure somebody with a rifle takes position in the second floor of the hotel. Have him cover the front of my office and the street."

"Gunter Wald can manage that," the blacksmith said.

"Can he shoot?"

"Well enough," Rex answered. "He can hit a shirt button at twenty-five paces with his Sharps rifle."

"In that case, make sure he chooses the right button when the time comes," Adam said. "Who else can we count on?"

"My apprentice will make the rounds and ask for volunteers. I'll send you the list once I get it."

Adam scanned the hills ringing Luther. Birds fluttered above the distant trees, and clouds floated by, majestic as ships. Violence seemed as unlikely as a volcano erupting.

"What'll be the signal to summon the posse?" Rex asked. "Too bad the church doesn't have a bell."

"When folks hear gunfire, they'll know to come. But don't rush to the jail. Hildon will be expecting that. Better to box him in." Adam tapped the stick on the corners at either end of the sketch. "As the posse gathers, have them take cover. Take advantage of the longer reach of your rifles and shotguns and pick Hildon's men off their saddles. If you can, have somebody sneak around behind the jail to cover the back door."

Eyes hooded and serious, Rex studied the map. "Where will you be if and when this mess starts?"

"Won't do any good to speculate. I'll be wherever I am when the devil makes his presence known."

Rex's wife had been watching, and she stepped outside her door. Rex's gaze shifted toward her. "Can't say I'm too happy about any of this," he said. He rubbed the deputy star on his vest. "My days of playing hero ended when an exploding shell knocked me flat at Gettysburg. And you shouldn't worry about me rushing to anything." He leaned on his cane to emphasize his point.

The clop of hooves and the rattle of a wagon drew their attention to the street. Edward Blair, the undertaker, drove a buckboard laden with a trunk and a folded canvas tent. Three men on horses rode alongside. Adam recognized the escort from the earlier posse that had chased after the Norman brothers and recovered the safe. The undertaker and his party were on the way to retrieve the remains of the late Sheriff Cook and Miss Francine Mills, which by this time should be good and ripe, if much remained beyond scattered bones, thanks to scavenging coyotes, bears, and ravens.

"That's four men we could use for the posse," Rex said.

"Hopefully we won't need them," Adam replied. "Just pass the word if the gang comes into town, be ready to fight."

Rex stared at Adam like he was reading him.

"Anything else on your mind?" Adam asked.

Rex cleared his throat and looked toward his shop. "Only that I have work to do." He turned his broad back to Adam and limped away.

The sun shone bright, yet Adam felt the clammy shadow of regret and trepidation. His nerves tingled with a distant alarm. He hoped time would pass without incident, that his fears would fade to nothing. Luther deserved peace and quiet, and he needed his spirit to loosen and let him breathe easier.

On the way back to his office, he surveyed the main street and etched in his mind its forlorn serenity. At any moment disaster in the form of Hildon Norman could return and shatter this tranquility. That bastard and his gang of killers would leave a wake of misery and death. Adam kicked a stone and sent it skipping down the street. How much of this worry was his fault?

What started this grief was the West brothers coming into town with their stolen money. Hell, even the sainted Sheriff Cook had made sure to grease his palm with the dirty cash. Maybe if Adam hadn't clipped a share for himself, Carruthers and the Normans would have no reason to slither this way. He swallowed hard. The dry, bitter ball of remorse refused to go down, reminding him that his playing the lingering ends of this crooked scheme could bring a lot of tears to the innocent people of this town.

He returned to his office and checked on the prisoners. Carruthers and Speight sat on opposite ends of the bunk, both men barefoot and stripped to their undergarments. Chains trailed from their ankles to the iron bars. Carruthers silently mouthed the words as he read a tattered newspaper. Speight lay back with his eyes closed, his shoulders and head against the wall. Both men looked as unkempt as mangy hounds. Adam paid the guard a dime and sent him back to his ranch.

Carruthers cut his gaze toward Adam. "Any chance of breakfast? Maybe sometime this month?"

"You ate last night. That should hold you a spell."

"When I'm hungry like this I get loud and ornery."

"Make all the goddamn noise you want; I'll feed you when I'm good and ready." Adam walked away. These two criminals could stew in their own fetid juices. Too bad he had to smell them.

Adam passed the day sorting what belonged to the office of the sheriff and what belonged to Nelson Cook. He collected Cook's belongings and personal correspondence in a box. Since he couldn't remember if Cook had ever mentioned any kin, Adam was forced to read his friend's letters, which filled him with guilt for prying into the dead man's private life. He perused correspondence, mostly from women, and when he stumbled across the mention of a sister, he gratefully stopped reading. After noting the return address on the envelope, he penned a letter to inform her of the unfortunate reasons for the greeting and that he would mail Cook's belongings when he heard back.

The next stagecoach from Rawlins wouldn't arrive for two days, and, if Adam was lucky, he'd hear then about his request for a trial. It could be weeks before this business with Carruthers was settled. Adam felt certain a jury would either hang Carruthers or lock him up in the penitentiary at Fort Leavenworth until his black heart gave out.

Besides the specter of Hildon's impending attack, Adam worried about the money hidden beneath his office floor. He hoped to be spared another crop of bad luck. After all he'd gone through on account of this cash, wouldn't it be the most shameful misfortune to have someone spot him taking the money, or for the office to burn down and incinerate his wealth?

The money nagged him, and he picked at this worry like a scab. He wanted to ride away but was tied by his duties and seemed to be as much a prisoner of this town as were Carruthers and Speight.

Sometime in the mid-afternoon he stopped Anderson's young son, who was passing by the office, and gave the boy a few coins to fetch lunch and refreshment from the Mountain View. After a meal of split pea soup and a slice of ham on bread plus coffee, Adam stepped to the doorway for fresh air. Times like this he wished he had taken up smoking, to distract him and help pass the day.

At the south end of the street, a man on a horse approached—a tawny gelding, the steady beat of its hooves raising dust clouds. The shadow from the man's hat masked his face, and, as he drew closer, Adam couldn't recognize him. A holster with a revolver flopped from the man's belt. He swept his gaze across the town, then set his eyes on Adam and rode straight toward him.

Adam made sure his badge was pinned right and his coat hung away from his pistols, leaving them accessible for quick action. He pushed away from the doorjamb and stepped across the wooden sidewalk to the street.

The rider wore clothes filthy with dust and boots spattered with dried mud. Yet he sat proud and menacing, like he was spoiling for trouble. This close, he looked sixteen. Eighteen at most. Face smooth as an apple, reddened by long days under this brutal sun. A kid foolish enough to be acting like a dangerous man when he should be learning a useful trade. He halted his horse and looked down on Adam. "You the sheriff?"

The young stranger's haughty manner and voice irritated Adam. "Wouldn't be wearing this badge if I wasn't." He rested his right hand firmly on the butt of his Colt revolver.

The rider grinned, glanced over his shoulder, and then back at Adam.

Who did the kid look at? Adam looked past the rider and studied the distant brush, grayed by haze. He didn't see anyone, but his suspicions remained sharp. *Maybe someone watching through a telescope. Or through the sights of a sharpshooter's rifle.*

Adam shifted his weight so he was light on both feet.

"Well, Sheriff—" the kid said.

"You wanna talk, get your ass off the horse."

The young man's mouth pursed, and he glared at Adam. He swung one leg over the back of the saddle and planted both of his boots in the hard-packed dirt. He stood as tall as Adam, and hard muscles filled his shirt. His eyes were blue-gray, like the air above the far horizon, and they shone with an arrogance this kid didn't deserve. "I got a message from Hildon Norman. It's about Brandon Carruthers."

Adam snorted. "I was hoping you wouldn't say that."

The kid beamed smugly. "Why?"

" 'Cause it means you're even more stupid than what you let on."

The insult made the kid's mouth flatten into a tight, angry line. His eyes crinkled into slits.

Adam stepped around him and studied the pastel mosaic of the shrubs and hills beyond the town limits. He pretended to ignore the kid, but, from the corner of his eye, he watched the young man turn to see what Adam was looking at.

Quick as a hawk, Adam whirled, drew his revolver, and cranked back the hammer. He grabbed the kid's arm and jammed the muzzle of the .45 into his side.

The kid tensed, and his jaw muscles rippled. His eyes swiveled and locked on Adam. "Goddamn you, Sheriff, when this is—"

Adam swept a boot and knocked the kid's legs out from under him. The kid fell on his back, stiffening in fear as Adam crouched beside him and poked the barrel of the Colt against his ribs.

"Hold still," Adam warned with a menacing whisper. He reached to unholster the kid's pistol, which he tossed aside.

Leaning into his revolver so the hard steel barrel pressed deep into the kid's chest, Adam scanned the confused tangle of brush in the distance, certain the gang would react.

His heartbeat marked the passing seconds. Nothing moved.

Except the kid. He flinched. Adam jammed the barrel even harder to keep him still.

After several more seconds of nothing happening, he hauled the kid upright and swung him around, then shoved him into the middle of the street in the direction from which he'd approached. "Now go find yourself another line of work."

The kid shuffled forward, both hands raised. "What about my horse?"

"It's been confiscated. You got a problem with that, petition the governor." Adam kicked the kid in the pants and sent him stumbling.

The kid shambled into the street. Faces appeared in the saloon door.

A puff of smoke burst in the tree line past the kid's shoulder. Adam dropped to the dirt. A bullet whined overhead and cracked into a wall down the street. The horse shrieked and raced away.

The shot had broken the tension. Adam sprang to his feet and scrambled toward the saloon, then spun back to the sheriff's office, trusting that reversing course bought him time. A second bullet ricocheted in the dirt. Another whirred past his ear. He raised his pistol and emptied the cylinder in quick shots, certain he wasn't doing much but sounding the alarm. Once inside the office, he would retrieve the Winchester and hold off Hildon's gang until Rex and the posse arrived.

Hopefully before those criminals shot the town to pieces.

Chapter Nineteen

Bullets clipped the ground around Adam's feet. Bursts of smoke rose from the thicket beyond the town. A man scrambled from one bush to the next, rifle in hand.

Adam dove through the doorway of his office and landed on the floor. Another volley of rifle bullets chewed the doorjamb. He lay flat and realized his hands were trembling. He clutched them into fists to hold them still.

His mind's eye pushed through the terror and ranged over the situation. Several riflemen in the woods. What about the kid? The last glimpse Adam had of him, he was running out of the line of fire and dropping to the sidewalk on the opposite side of the street from the sheriff's office.

Adam cursed himself for reacting as he had to the kid. Rather than humiliate and send him away, Adam should've cuffed and interrogated him. Learned Hildon's plan. How many men were in the attack party? Hildon. Bigotes, the big Mexican with the cruel eyes. Those two miscreants for sure. Plus a couple of others who'd ambushed Adam before the cavalry arrived. Maybe more, for all Adam knew.

How fast would the call to action echo from the town to the ranches and farms? Rex should be here soon. With luck he'd bring three, four men with rifles and shotguns to even the odds. Hopefully, they'd arrive with enough grit to pursue the fight.

Adam swallowed hard, set his mind to action, and leapt up from the floor. He snatched the Winchester from the wall rack and slung the leather bandolier over his head and one shoulder. He cocked the rifle and tucked it under his arm, then fished a box of pistol cartridges from a desk drawer and dumped fistfuls of loose rounds into his pockets. As he hustled past the jail cell toward the back door, he replaced the spent cartridges in his revolver. Discarded shells clattered on the floor by his boots.

Carruthers clung to the iron bars of the cell. Speight's eyes gleamed rat-like from under the bunk where he'd sought shelter. The older outlaw watched Adam with the eager expression of a caged animal certain escape was imminent. "Hey, Sheriff, you're running around like your tail is on fire." He started to laugh, and his disturbing howl filled the back room.

Adam ignored the maniacal outburst. His revolver reloaded and the empty loops of his gun belt replenished, he lifted the bar from the back door and cracked it open, then peeked through the sliver of light.

A bullet hit the door. He slammed it closed, retreating as another slug punched through the thick panels. Splinters flecked against his coat.

Carruthers spoke, still chortling. "There ain't nowhere to run, you dumb son of a bitch. Hold me a seat when you get to hell."

All the saliva evaporated from Adam's mouth. Just as he'd predicted, Hildon's crew had covered the back door to trap him. What next? Climb on the roof like they'd done before? Or take hostages?

A bullet zinged through a front wall and pinged against the iron bars. Speight whimpered and slid farther beneath the bunk. Carruthers only laughed louder.

More bullets punched through the front and back walls. Shafts of light lanced through the holes. Adam crouched for cover in the doorway between the back room and the office while Carruthers guffawed and hopped through the glowing swirls of dust, oblivious to the lead slugs smacking around him.

Gunfire boomed loud, close. The office window shattered. Bullets traced straight lines through the room, revealing that these shooters were in front of the sheriff's office. The attack was simple and deadly—an anvil and hammer assault. The man covering the back door was the anvil, the men in the street, the hammer. And with each passing moment, the space between hammer and anvil grew smaller and smaller.

Carruthers slapped the iron bars in spastic glee. Blood trickled from a bullet nick on his arm, but he kept laughing and cursing.

When would the posse arrive? Adam's plan had sounded so practical when he thought it up. But the townsmen were scattered all over. At best it would take a half hour for them to assemble. Adam had only seconds. The bullet-ridden front door swung on its hinges. The window curtains hung in tattered rags. Waiting until a bullet found him wasn't any kind of strategy. Cold fury gave him new strength. Hildon and his gang were going to eat their share of lead. Adam eased onto the office floor belly down and lizard-crawled through broken glass.

The shooting stopped, but the echo of gunfire remained in his ears. Training the rifle toward the window, he slowly raised his head.

He heard the scuffing of boots. The creaking of boards.

Adam rested his finger on the trigger and primed his nerves.

Carruthers yelled from his cell. "What are you yellow bastards waiting for? He's alone. Come get him."

The outline of a man's head with a hat darkened one of the curtains. The end of a rifle muzzle slipped under the curtain like it was sniffing for prey. Adam aimed at the shadow just above the rifle and fired.

The rifle tipped up, catching the curtain, revealing one of the shootists with blood spattered across his throat. His face was a grotesque mask of agony, and he staggered backwards and fell.

A fresh barrage of gunfire ripped through the wall. Splinters rained on Adam. He levered his Winchester and scooted sideways.

Men shouted outside. Guns were reloaded. Carruthers quit laughing, perhaps sensing that his rescue had stalled. Adam hadn't heard horses, so, apart from the kid he'd shamed, he guessed Hildon and crew were on foot.

He'd counted at least two guns shooting from the street. If he surprised them, he could hit one, then duck back under cover.

Crawling forward, he drew himself close to the front door and folded his legs to pop up into a firing position. He tossed his hat aside. Once exposed, he'd have no more than a second to aim and shoot before the desperadoes returned fire.

He listened and waited. Heard only the rustle of clothing. He firmed his grip on the Winchester, tensed his legs, and lunged upward into the doorway.

His mind froze the image in his retinas. Four men approached his office. Closest to him, a big man Adam didn't recognize who aimed a Henry repeater. Then Hildon with a Spencer carbine, limping, putting weight on his good leg. Next to him, Bigotes. And the kid, holding a pistol in each hand. They stood in a loose formation, ten feet apart from one another. Their gazes panned the office and, as one, locked on him.

He reacted through instinct. Adam snapped his sights on the big man and fired.

The big man slumped forward and dropped. Bigotes let loose a string of quick shots, hazing the air with smoke.

Hildon fired. The bullet hacked into the doorframe. Adam felt the pressure of the round striking the wood, and his body recoiled. He pushed away, right back into the open.

Bigotes shuffled backwards as he ejected spent cartridges from his revolver. The kid worked his thumbs over the hammers of his guns, alternating pistols as he fired. Smoke chugged from their muzzles. But his shots were hurried and clumsy, zinging harmlessly past Adam.

He raced Hildon to see who could first chamber a new round and shoot. Adam swung the lever of his Winchester. It jammed. His heart caught in panic. He tried to force the lever but it held. A spent cartridge had snagged in the ejection port. Mind racing at lightning speed, Adam dropped the rifle and reached for one of his Colts.

Hildon swung his rifle lever closed and drew a bead. Adam knew he had lost.

A shot rang through the street. Hildon's legs buckled, and he sank to his knees in the dirt.

The kid glanced at Hildon, and his face blanched with shock. He lowered his pistols and sprinted away up the road.

Thunderous gunfire shook the air. A swarm of bullets churned the dirt street into a cloud of dust. The kid got about ten feet before he fell. Bullets ricocheted past Adam as he hopped back through the doorway into his office.

Hildon and the kid lay crumpled in the street. Dust tufted around their fallen bodies.

Someone yelled, "Stop your shooting!"

The staccato gunshots slowed, then faded to silence. Adam waited a moment, then slowly rose to his feet.

An arm waved through the gun smoke obscuring the windows on the second floor of the Mountain View. Adam waved back. He stepped outside.

Hildon, the kid, and the stranger remained in bloody heaps. Two men were missing: Bigotes and the shooter behind the jail.

At the south end of the street, a familiar shape limped into view. Burt Rex. Two other men appeared beside him. All carried long guns.

Townspeople crept from the doorways along Main Street.

They paused on the sidewalk, looking unconvinced that the violence had stopped for good.

Rex and his two companions approached. Adam holstered his pistols and retrieved the Winchester. He pawed at the stuck cartridge until it shucked free. A sudden thirst parched his throat. He walked into the street to greet his deputy.

Gunter Wald strode out of the Mountain View. He cradled a Sharps rifle, and a cartridge belt was slung around his waist. With the back of a hand, he brushed aside a thin lock of hair from his tall forehead.

Wald, Rex, and the other two shooters gathered around Adam and stared at the dead men. Wald tried to smile, but his eyes showed strained relief, not triumph. "Truth be told, I've never shot a man before. I don't even like hunting."

Rex tapped Hildon's body with his boot. "If there was anyone who deserved shooting, it was him."

Wald whispered, "But it was me who killed him."

Adam swung his gaze across the street, to the lingering smoke, to the faces that studied him. His defensive plan had worked, though he felt no satisfaction. He wondered what would be happening if it were him dead in the dirt. Weariness pulled at his bones, and he wanted to sit somewhere and rest.

Two riders on horses rounded the corner at the far end of the street. The first horse pulled a rope that dragged a corpse by its ankles. As the riders came closer, Adam recognized them as two of the undertaker's escort. The body towed behind them belonged to a man from Hildon's gang.

"We didn't get far when we heard the shooting. So we doubled back. Didn't figure Sheriff Cook and Miss Mills are going to mind waiting. Hope that's not a problem." The rider lashed the rope against the corpse and his voice turned grim. "Caught this rascal making tracks from behind your office."

A dozen more men and horses galloped into the street. They

assembled around Adam, all of them brandishing guns and looking disappointed that the fight was over.

The mood among the people was uneven. Those who missed the shootout appeared ready to celebrate victory over the gang. Those like himself and Gunter Wald, who had a hand in the killing, were unsettled and withdrawn.

"Is this it?" one of the townspeople asked, a ranch hand Adam recognized but didn't know by name.

"I think they got their fill of trouble," he replied. "Even stupid men like them know when they got whipped." He looked over the assembled crowd and selected a team of men to take the bodies to the undertaker's, then dismissed the rest and returned to his office. Just inside the door, he picked up his hat, brushed dust and wood splinters from the brim, and put it on. Exhausted and queasy, all he wanted was to sit in his chair and brood over what had happened.

One thought pricked him. Bigotes had escaped.

He considered leading the posse out to hunt that killer until they cornered him. Adam pictured Bigotes snarling like a treed mountain lion, as good as dead once he'd been caught. But going after Bigotes might strain Adam's luck past the breaking point. Better to accept this victory and hope the mustached outlaw had disappeared for good.

To keep himself busy and dark thoughts at bay, he found a broom and a dustpan and swept up the broken glass and debris. A short while later, Rex came by with whiskey. Adam asked him to brew coffee instead. He had to think straight until his mind cleared and his stomach uncurdled.

During the next two days, Adam hired a crew to help him guard the prisoners and repair the damage to his office. He mounted a horse and ranged through the hills surrounding Luther, mindful that Bigotes was alive. Hopefully, that *desgraciado* had had enough and moved on to easier pickings.

With so many folks occupied over him, Adam had to postpone plans to recover the money stashed beneath the floorboards. The stagecoach from Rawlins rumbled into town, but the usual hubbub surrounding its arrival was muted. The mail included a dispatch from the territorial judicial district appointing a judge—no name given—to preside over the trial of Brandon Carruthers and Morgan Speight.

Adam put the dispatch away and ordered dinner for his two prisoners. Carruthers slurped his stew with heavy grimness, his morose expression acknowledging that his fate was certain. He couldn't hope for a long stay behind bars. No, men like him were meant to die at the end of a short stretch of rope. Speight finished his meal with an equally bleak expression.

The following day Edward Blair returned with the remains of Cook and Francine, wrapped in separate muslin sacks. As expected, the scavengers hadn't left much. The next day the town turned out for the funeral.

Since he had known Cook the longest, Adam had the painful duty of delivering the eulogy. During the war, he had gotten much practice burying soldiers who had died too young. Most times it was men he didn't know, but once in a while it was someone he had broken bread with. When it was Adam's turn to share a few thoughts about the honored dead, the words would knot inside his throat, and the harder he tried to dislodge them, the more the effort would make his eyes water as a terrible despair raked through him.

Now, Adam's vision blurred with those familiar tears. He'd already given one eulogy for Cook, back when he'd found the sheriff and Francine after they'd been murdered. Adam couldn't remember the words he'd said then but recalled what he felt at the time: sorrow and revenge. With the capture of Brandon Carruthers and Morgan Speight and the deaths of others in the Hildon gang, the yearning for vengeance had faded but did little to weaken the desolation of loss. What Adam wanted to do more than anything else was fall to his knees and sob and mourn the death of someone he'd regarded as close as a brother.

Staring toward the distant horizon, Adam tried his best to speak in a calm voice. "It is at an occasion like this when I have to acknowledge that I will never be as righteous as I'm supposed to be. To be sure, Sheriff Nelson Cook had his failings, as we all do, but he was a shining light in my life. He made me want to be a better man, to be worthy of the soul God has bestowed within all of us."

The ache welled, and Adam fell silent. Try as he might, he couldn't think of anything but his sorrow. Eyes fixed upon him, as if waiting for him to crack. Then he remembered Nelson's scheme for his share of the loot, and the thought brought a warmth that Adam kept to himself.

He continued, more composed now. "Throughout his life, Sheriff Cook had to scratch and scramble to keep food in his belly, clothes on his back, and a horse beneath him. He was no different than the rest of us in these hard times, and we can't fault him for making the compromises we all make to smooth the grit and rough edges of life. I'll never be mistaken for a learned man, but the war did make me memorize one item of Scripture, simply because I heard it recited so often for those on their way to meet our Maker. It is from Isaiah, Chapter 44, Verse 22: *'I have swept away your offenses like a cloud, your sins like the morning mist. Return to me, for I have redeemed you.'* "

As Adam spoke, a random breeze stirred the grass and weeds and brushed dust over the open graves.

"And so, Nelson Cook, soldier, sheriff, patriot, friend, we bid you goodbye until we embrace again in the heavenly afterlife." Adam paused a beat. "Amen."

The crowd mumbled in reply: "Amen."

Little was said over Francine other than God rest her soul.

Afterwards everyone else save for the undertaker's hired hand gathered in the Mountain View Saloon and Hotel for a wake; Adam stayed behind to help shovel dirt onto Cook's coffin.

Definitely a low point in a man's life, he thought, *burying your best friend.*

When he was done, he stared at the mound of dirt that marked the final resting place of Sheriff Nelson Cook. He wanted to say something, even wished he could pray, but words refused to come. Adam returned to his office, washed the sweat off his face, and diluted his grief with whiskey.

In the middle of the following week a loud commotion broke the afternoon calm.

A column of mounted cavalry, in blue coats with bright yellow stripes and matching shoulder braids, rode into town. Instead of wide-brimmed hats, the men wore black Prussian-style helmets with glittering brass eagles fixed to their fronts. The golden plumes on their helmets bobbed in cadence with the trotting horses.

Adam felt his eyebrows rise as he appraised the spectacle. Out on the frontier, cavalrymen tended to look as rough as tree stumps. These troopers looked as pretty as toy soldiers fresh out a box. Plus, there wasn't an Indian scout or buffalo soldier among them.

An officer rode in the lead, followed by two flag bearers, one with a cavalry pennant and the other with a blue regimental standard. A stagecoach traveled in the middle of the contingent.

The officer shouted a command. The troop turned smartly in the middle of the street and formed two lines facing the Mountain View. The coach proceeded to the entrance of the saloon and halted. Dust hung in the air.

A parade like this was worthy of a senator. Or a governor. Adam smirked as he thought, *or a judge.*

He made sure his shirt was buttoned, buffed his badge, and walked out of his office. He passed through the middle of the formation, politely excusing himself when he brushed against their polished boots and fine horses. He waited between the saloon door and the stagecoach. Around him, townspeople flocked like birds and chattered in speculation.

The coach's interior remained in shadow. Adam saw the silhouettes of four passengers, and he smelled tobacco smoke.

A sergeant riding shotgun on the coach climbed down, placed a step beneath the coach door, opened it, and then stood ramrod straight and clicked his boot heels. Adam found himself wanting to stand at attention, too, but decided to simply square his shoulders and offer a handshake. After all, he was no longer a soldier, and this was his town.

A man descended backwards out the door, his broad back clad in a frock coat. His shoes groped for the step, and, as his weight shifted, the coach swayed. He paused to don a black top hat. Gray hair bunched along the back of his collar. He let go of a handgrip, turned around, and stepped aside to let another passenger dismount. A woman's face appeared in the sunlight over the door.

Adam's curiosity flashed into astonishment.

His hand went to his wallet and the letter inside. He recognized the man and the woman. Judge Gideon Buchanan and the judge's daughter, Tess.

Two people Adam thought he'd never see again.

Chapter Twenty

Tess Buchanan winced the instant she recognized Adam Sanchez. When she read the letter directing her father to preside over a murder trial in Luther, Wyoming, she'd felt a prickle of dismay upon seeing Adam's name.

At the time, she thought, *could it be* that *Adam Sanchez?* The same man she'd spurned years ago? The charming rogue who seemed to have no more lofty aims in life than avoiding a steady job?

At her father's urging, she had pushed Adam away for a gentleman more suited to the daughter of a federal judge. Now Tess had arrived in this dusty knot of buildings, back at her father's side as a court clerk, divorced and disgraced by a thieving, philandering husband. A blue-blood Harvard man, no less.

The sergeant beside the stagecoach took Tess's hand and helped her onto the wooden sidewalk. Her eyes remained on Adam and caught the fleeting surprise that colored his face when he noticed her.

Yes, it was that Adam Sanchez. *Sheriff* Adam Sanchez. Tess wondered how he had evolved from wandering scoundrel to upstanding lawman.

Adam's gaze shifted from her to her father, Judge Gideon Buchanan. Tess remembered Adam was a bit of dandy even though he lived out of a saddlebag. Not surprisingly, as a keeper of the law with a permanent residence, he was well turned out. Pressed frock coat. Starched collar. Brushed hat. A recent haircut and shave. Polished sheriff's star. For her part, Tess felt the sweat and grime of the journey from Cheyenne and imagined herself filthy as a horse blanket.

The third passenger in the coach, the prosecutor Frederick Jackson, a well-dressed sort with a trimmed goatee, climbed out and dumped a heavy leather satchel by his feet. The last passenger, Pierre Hollande, advocate for the accused, emerged from the coach. The judge's detachment commander, an army captain regal as a peacock, stepped onto the sidewalk.

A cluster of locals introduced themselves. Gunter Wald, proprietor of the Mountain View Hotel and Saloon. Daryl Anderson, who owned the town mercantile. His wife, Gloria, a sociable and attractive woman who laughed a little too flirtatiously at a comment from the captain. An Oriental woman named Lucy, who stood at Gloria's side, also greeted them.

Both her father and Adam pretended they were meeting for the first time. She wanted to laugh out loud at the overwrought social mores that kept them living according to a melodramatic script. Adam acknowledged Tess with a polite nod, then averted his eyes. She wasn't hurt by his tepid manner. They all had their public roles to play . . . he as the professional constable and she as level-headed clerk and secretary to her father.

But she couldn't deny the ache that had tormented her all these years whenever she remembered Adam and regretted spurning him. On the bumpy stagecoach ride she'd tried to lose herself in a book of poems and essays, but her heart kept wandering to memories of Adam and the promise of what their life could've been. He was here now, and what would happen? What *could* happen? What did she want to happen? Gloria invited everyone into the saloon. The cool air smelled moist and soapy from the freshly mopped floor. Tess glanced back to make sure Adam followed them in.

Her father strutted into the center of the saloon. He dropped his hat on a table, slicked back his thinning gray hair, and scratched his beard. He tucked his hands into the pockets of his waistcoat and pivoted to assess the darkening room. Lucy dragged a stepladder through the saloon and climbed it to light the ceiling lanterns. He asked, "Is this the largest venue in Luther?"

"It is," replied Daryl. "We hold town meetings here."

Her father pulled a chair out from a table and sat facing the bar. "Then this saloon will do. Not the most distinguished place for a court of law but at least we're conveniently close to libations."

"We have whiskey." Daryl swept his hand across the bottles racked on the wall behind the bar. "Wine. Beer."

"Ice?" the judge asked.

"Plenty of blocks in the cellar," Daryl replied.

Her father knitted his fingers over his substantial belly and stretched his legs. "Excellent. If you have sarsaparilla, then mix it with bourbon and serve it over ice. It's a popular concoction from New Orleans called a cock-tail. Most refreshing."

Tess held up a finger and addressed the barkeep. "The judge will have *one*."

Her father chuckled. "In your tallest glass. And be generous with the whiskey. The dusty ride here has provoked an intense thirst."

Jackson dropped the satchel by the judge's chair, opened it, and retrieved folders, a ledger, and documents bound in ribbon that he spread across the table. "Your Honor," Adam inquired, "would you like to see the accused men? They're in the jail across the street."

Her father pushed the legal papers back to clear space in front of him. "There's no rush. I'll meet them at their arraignment." He pulled a cigar and a box of lucifers from inside his coat pocket. He struck a lucifer, lit the cigar, and blew smoke across the documents.

Tess considered the stacks of paper and thought about all the work waiting for her attention. The trial. Keeping her father sober enough to act as judge. And what was she going to do about Adam?

Her face grew warm, and she dropped her gaze to the floor to avoid looking at him.

Adam wanted to stare at Tess but knew better. He breathed deep and tried to slough off the excitement at seeing her so unexpectedly. He wanted to compare his memory of her to the reality of her physical presence. Her bulky travel garments—a cape thrown back to reveal a loose jacket, a billowing skirt—seemed to draw attention to her trim physique rather than hide it. The intervening years had etched tiny crow's feet at the corners of her large, brown eyes but did nothing to detract from the elegant lines of her face. Her hands looked as graceful as before. He remembered how her touch caressed his skin under the covers on cool mornings. That same tangle of brunette hair spilling from under her hat used to brush his face when they kissed. Her keepsake letter in his pocket seemed to gain weight. A hole opened in his heart, and through it rushed emotions that he wished had remained locked away.

Judge Buchanan appeared in no hurry to start the business of the trial, so there was little point in Adam remaining in the saloon and torturing his mind with Tess's presence. He dismissed himself and, on the way out the door, wondered if the awkwardness between her and him was as obvious as the gathering coolness of the evening.

Once outside the saloon, he hustled to his office and shut the door. By the glow of a lamp in the back room, he could see one of Rex's hired hands guarding the prisoners. The fellow put down a gazette he'd been reading. Carruthers and Speight were doing their usual. Sleeping and stinking. Adam checked to make sure the cell and back door were secure, then paid the guard ten cents and sent him away.

Adam returned to his desk and lit the reading lamp, then took off his gun belt and draped it across the back of his chair. He sat and wondered about Tess. Now that she was in Luther, he would've preferred the trial be moved to Rawlings. That way he would only see her when he appeared to testify. But, with the trial here, they'd be rubbing shoulders and trading looks practically on an hourly basis. To see her so frequently, after all this time, would chafe the wounds in his spirit.

When the trial was over, Tess and her father would leave. Carruthers and Speight would either hang or be sent to prison. Either way, they'd be out of his hair. Adam could then put his mind to retrieving the ten thousand dollars from under the floorboards and finding a way to stash that loot where he could safely spend it. But Tess would linger in his heart.

Someone knocked on the office door. Adam figured it was the detachment captain, or his sergeant, or the clerk coming to ask about a logistical matter. "Come in."

It was Tess who entered. All the feelings Adam struggled to keep bottled up gushed through him. Though he should've stood to greet her, he remained seated, overwhelmed with emotion and paralyzed by indecision.

She had removed her cloak. Her jacket was unbuttoned and framed a striped blouse yellow with dust. She placed a cardboard parcel on his desk. "This arrived for you in the mail." She said it matter of factly, as if this package were the only business between them.

Adam turned an inquisitive gaze on the parcel. It was the size of a small book, and he picked it up to inspect the label. The parcel was addressed to *Sheriff, Luther, Wyoming*, with the return address of *Carrillo & Smith Photography Studio, Cheyenne*. He set the parcel down.

"Open it, please," she implored. "I'm just as curious as you are."

He searched the top drawer for a penknife that he used to slice open the cardboard packaging. He removed another package wrapped in a layer of heavy paper and, under that, tissue. Tess leaned close. He kept his eyes on the package, but her proximity sharpened his other senses. Her clothes rustled. She brought an earthy and floral aroma of perspiration mixed with perfume. He was certain he could feel the heat of her skin. He cut the paper tape binding the tissue to reveal a daguerreotype set in a gilded frame.

From behind the layer of glass, a sepia-tone version of Nelson Cook stared solemnly at the camera as if conveying the impression of a man of great importance. He sat stiffly on a wingback chair, left hand resting on one of the arms, right hand holding a Remington revolver on his lap. He wore a frock coat and a matching derby, cocked to one side to keep any shadow off his face. His mustache was trim and his sideburns neat from a recent haircut, likely so he'd look his best for posterity. A sheriff's badge shone on the lapel of his coat, and a watch chain drooped across his vest.

Adam blinked at the image as though his friend had come to life. He now wore that same badge, taken from Cook's corpse. Grief wet Adam's eyes. He laid the frame on the desk for Tess to see.

She picked it up. "Sheriff Cook?"

Adam wiped his nose and fought back tears. "The late Sheriff Nelson Cook. A better man never lived." He knew that wasn't true, but he felt better saying it. He noticed a wedding ring on Tess's finger, and his sadness evaporated, replaced by a hard shell of cynicism. If Tess was married, why should he wring his heart over a love that was over with long ago? He felt foolish and clenched his jaw in anger. He wanted to snatch her letter from his pocket, rip it to shreds, and toss the scraps in the stove.

"You were friends?" she asked.

"Good friends," he replied coldly. "He deserved better."

She rested the daguerreotype on the desk. "I read your deposition." Her gaze roved across his office and loitered on the plaster-filled bullet holes in the walls and ceiling, then shifted to the scorch marks on the furniture, then to the mismatched, repaired floorboards. "The men who murdered Cook and Francine Mills are vicious animals."

Adam shushed her. "Don't antagonize them," he whispered, cocking a thumb toward the doorway to the jail. "They're likely to say nasty words that will upset you." Then he realized how foolish that sounded. If she could talk so coolly of reading the ugly details he'd written, a few cuss words weren't likely to distress her. "If you want to talk, we're going to need some privacy."

He slipped one of his revolvers from the gun belt and tucked it into the waistband of his trousers. Then he stood and led Tess out the front door, which he closed behind them. They stood beneath the awning over the sidewalk. The light shining through the office window illuminated her face and made her eyes sparkle. She buttoned her jacket against the night's chill and leaned against one of the awning posts. Though no one else was around or apparently within earshot, Adam knew the Luther gossip circle would soon be wagging its tongue with speculation about him and Tess.

Adam propped himself against the wall between the window and door where he could watch her and the street, and listen for any commotion in the jail. She kept quiet, yet he could tell she had much to say. He wasn't sure he wanted to hear it. But the silence between them grew uncomfortable, and he decided to clear the air.

"I find it strange that your father is presiding at this trial. In his last words to me, he said the West was a wilderness fit only for vagabonds, heathens, and savages. Or similar words. I didn't commit them to memory." Adam didn't give her a chance to respond before asking, "Where is your husband?"

Tess's eyes crinkled. She held up her left hand, fingers extended. "One reason I wear this ring is to remind me of a bad decision I once made."

"Is that why you're here? To revisit those bad decisions? Or to ease your troubled soul? I should warn you, either way I'm not much of a confessor."

"I don't need absolution, especially from someone with a reputation like yours." Tess lowered her hand. "Being a sheriff doesn't wipe your slate clean. I'm surprised to see you here." She inhaled deeply, shifted her weight, and exhaled. "Truth is, both my father and I made some unfortunate choices. If you want to hear an apology for what happened between us, here it is."

Adam felt foolish, realizing he must've sounded like a petulant child. He raised a hand. "You owe me nothing."

A smile floated on her lips, then disappeared.

"If you've come here for truth," he said, "then I must reply in kind." He readied himself for the next words. "I've missed you very much."

Her smile returned and this time it didn't disappear as quickly. She whispered, "I missed you, too." She slipped the wedding ring from her finger and tucked it in a jacket pocket. "I'm divorced. The other reason I wear the ring is to keep men from assuming I'm available."

He stared, trying to read her face. Did her removing the ring mean she was available? To him?

"Isn't it funny how fate turns back on itself?" she asked.

"Are you talking about us?"

"And my father. He borrowed a lot of money to speculate on a railroad and lost everything. Criminals should learn how to run banks rather than rob them. That way they get rewarded for their chicanery instead of facing a life behind bars." Tess pushed away from the post and sat on a bench next to the door of the sheriff's office. "I doubt my father will ever restore his name or earn the money he needs to pay what he owes. He's a fine judge. And a better drunk. But he's no businessman. Despite what he once declared about the West, he swallowed what was left of his pride and accepted this posting in exchange for forgiveness of some of his debts."

"That's his story," Adam said. "What brings you here?"

"My former husband, the whore-mongering bastard, left me penniless and humiliated. I accompany my father for a meager stipend and to keep him from wrecking what's left of his career."

Adam reflected on his situation and wanted to laugh at the irony. Tess and her father were the impoverished vagabonds now, while he had a home. And he—a comanchero, of all things—was held in regard by a community that respected him. If he was careful and clever, he might also have a lot of money in his pocket. But, more than that, he might yet have the only woman he truly loved.

Chapter Twenty-One

Tess had worried that the court wouldn't be able to find twelve jurors, but, as this was Wyoming, women could serve. Adam Sanchez had sent deputies to every ranch, farm, and homestead in the county. People proved eager to do their duty, most likely because the trial and the likelihood of a double hanging were sensational diversions from the monotony of daily chores.

Her father convened court in the saloon. A dining table served as his bench. Jackson and Hollande interviewed prospective jurors and by midmorning had selected twelve willing citizens. Her father stayed reasonably sober and kept the proceedings on track. Tess and Jackson worked at a table to his right, Hollande at his left. Serving as court reporter, she was to document the proceedings and had arrayed pens and a fresh bottle of ink beside her ledger.

Gunter Wald had to borrow chairs to accommodate everyone who wanted a seat in the improvised courtroom. Even so, the overflow crowded the back and sides of the room. Despite a welcome breeze wafting through the open windows, women were already fanning themselves.

Judge Buchanan savored a long puff on his cigar, then flicked away its ash and ground the still smoldering butt into a metal saucer. He waved away the smoke obscuring his face. "In light of the packed room, smoking will be forbidden during these proceedings."

The accused—Brandon Carruthers, known as the Silver Fox,

and his accomplice Morgan Speight—sat in two sturdy chairs before the judge's bench. They were handcuffed, and their ankles were bound in chains with only enough slack to let them shuffle about. A pair of cavalry troopers stood behind them. The detachment captain watched from the audience. The rest of his soldiers were patrolling the town.

Tess readied her pen as Mr. Jackson called Adam Sanchez. He cut a fine figure as he walked to the front of the room, which only sharpened her regret at what they'd lost.

Adam was the first witness. He paid attention to the oath as he was sworn in. *To tell the truth, the whole truth, and nothing but the truth.* As best as he could remember, or chose to remember.

Jackson waved a slip of paper and handed it to Adam. "Sheriff Sanchez, do you recognize this?"

The sight of it raised cold anger in him. "I do," Adam replied. "It is the note I recovered from Sheriff Nelson Cook's body."

"Where was the note?"

"In his vest pocket."

"Could you read it, please?"

Adam cleared his throat. He started, then halted when his tongue knotted around what he had to say. He cleared his throat again and read aloud. Though he tried to keep his tone flat and even, his voice cracked a bit when he recited the note's final words, ". . . this wretch Nelson Cook."

A horrified gasp rippled through the jurors and the rest of the courtroom. Even Judge Buchanan grimaced.

Jackson beckoned for the note. Adam handed it back to him, glad to be rid of the thing. Jackson stepped toward Carruthers and brandished the note. "This is damning evidence of your culpability in the murder of Sheriff Cook."

Hollande jumped to his feet. "Your Honor, there is no proof Mr. Carruthers wrote that note."

Adam drew breath but kept quiet. *Then who did?*

Carruthers's chains rattled as he shifted in his seat. His gaze ranged across the audience and the jury, his thick eyebrows levering one way, then the other as his forehead wrinkled. He sat straight in the chair and gave the judge a sideways look. "I won't deny I wrote that."

Another collective gasp took hold of the room. Hollande shook his head and sat back down. Tess paused in mid-sentence, the tip of her pen quivering over the pages of the court record. She regarded Carruthers for a moment, then dipped her pen in the bottle of ink and transcribed into the court record what this killer had just admitted.

Jackson pointed to an army map pinned to the wall next to the witness chair. "Sheriff Sanchez, could you tell the court where and in what condition you discovered the bodies?"

Adam turned in his seat to view the map. "Can I get up and take a closer look?"

"You may, sir," Jackson answered.

Adam stood and leaned close to the map as he searched for the Sweetwater Mountains. Upon finding them, he ran a finger over the map as he hunted for the basin he had crossed going north to reach Carruthers's camp in the Rattlesnake Hills. He tapped the map. "Right about here."

"And the condition of the bodies?"

The words clotted in Adam's throat. He coughed to shake them loose. He spoke mechanically, sparing few of the lurid details, noting that Francine Mills was naked and covered with marks of torture. Both she and Cook had been hanged and gut shot.

To help himself stay centered, Adam fixed his stare at a point high on the back wall. When he blinked and let his eyes relax, he noticed how quiet the room had become. Everyone was leaning forward in their seats, their attention riveted upon him.

Even Tess was letting spellbound curiosity show through her professional indifference.

"Had Miss Francine Mills been defiled?" Jackson asked.

"Objection," Hollande called out. "The prosecution is leading the witness."

"Sustained," Buchanan replied.

Jackson rocked on his heels. "Very well." He glanced at his notes on the table and said to the judge, "Your Honor, the court has established that the motive for all this mayhem and vile behavior was the money stolen from the First National Bank of Kansas." Jackson directed his attention back to Adam. "Sheriff, what happened to that money?"

Adam felt a different kind of knot form in his throat. He had to be careful with his reply. "After I recovered the money from Carruthers's gang, which was stored in saddlebags attached to a pony, I unfortunately lost the money again when the pony fell into a hole in the river we were fording. The saddlebags were washed away."

"And you made no attempt to recover the money?"

"I never had the opportunity. I didn't notice the saddlebags were missing until we reached the other side of the river."

Jackson stroked his bearded chin. "Let me repeat. You made no attempt to recover the money?"

"The river was rough and treacherous enough. Besides," Adam pointed to Carruthers and Speight, "bringing these fugitives to justice was my priority."

Jackson pivoted and returned to his chair at the table. "I have no further questions of this witness, Your Honor."

Buchanan tipped his head toward Hollande. "Counselor?"

Hollande stood. "I have no questions."

With that, Adam was excused from the witness chair. He took a place at one side of the room, against the wall and next to a window where he could breathe in the fresh air.

Jackson requested that Morgan Speight be summoned. The accused shambled forward, head down, chains dragging and rattling across the floor. His expression appeared withdrawn and pensive, while the quivering at his temples and the corners of his mouth revealed the turmoil roiling within.

The instant he put his hand on the Bible, his façade broke, and he scarcely managed to finish the oath as he crumpled in the chair, face clasped in both hands as he blubbered like a wretch. "It was Carruthers," he insisted between sobs, "that ordered the rest of us to string up the woman and the sheriff."

Hollande's expression grew pinched, and he rubbed his temples as he recognized the futility of defending Speight.

"Who shot them?" Jackson asked.

Speight lifted his red, teary eyes. "It was Plutarco Gonzales."

"Who?"

"The Mexican with the big mustache."

Adam allowed himself a small smile. *So that's Bigotes's true name. Plutarco Gonzales. I prefer Bigotes.*

"Why didn't you stop him?" Jackson pressed.

Speight stared at the prosecutor. "What kind of a question is that? Carruthers wanted them shot. Gonzales wanted to do the shooting. You'd have more luck stopping a fresh wound from bleeding."

"And Francine Mills was more than shot, wasn't she?"

Speight shrank from the question.

"You are to answer," Judge Buchanan demanded.

"She was—" Speight knitted his fingers so hard, they whitened. "She was—"

"Was what?" Jackson insisted.

"Violated," Speight replied, his voice meek.

A murmur of disgust coursed through the room.

"By whom?" Jackson asked.

"By the others," Speight insisted.

Judge Buchanan scowled. "And you did nothing?"

Speight rose from his seat, straining against his handcuffs. The soldiers on either side of him readied themselves to pounce. Speight regarded them and sat back down. He gestured at Carruthers. "He would've killed me and left me dangling beside the woman and the sheriff. That would've spared me the torture of this shame."

Carruthers wiped his nose and shrugged.

"So the two murders and the defilement of Miss Mills were at the direction of Brandon Carruthers?" Jackson asked.

"Yes," Speight said, tears again flooding his eyes.

Jackson ended his questioning and sat back down. During his turn to interview Speight, Hollande tried to get him to recant, but Speight continued to wallow in his remorse. Even if it was sincere, Adam figured Speight's true goal was to offer testimony against his boss in hopes of trading a noose for prison.

"The witness is excused," Buchanan ordered.

Speight slunk from the witness chair, an embarrassment to look at.

Jackson interviewed more witnesses, among them Burt Rex, Gunter Wald, Lucy, and Gloria Anderson, who recounted the incident when the alleged criminals first came to town and then the recent shootout. He read aloud an affidavit from the lieutenant commending the buffalo soldiers for their intervention to save Adam from the rest of Carruthers's gang. He also read a warrant issued for the arrest of Brandon Carruthers for crimes committed elsewhere, including armed robbery of the First National Bank of Kansas. At this last, Buchanan growled, "The jury will dismiss any mention of those charges. The testimony in this court will be limited solely to the circumstances involving the murders of Sheriff Nelson Cook and Francine Mills."

The trial continued through lunch. During closing arguments, Jackson simply recited the facts as presented. Hollande paced in front of the jurors and pled his case for the defendants, all the while wringing his hands. A noble but futile effort, Adam thought, because Carruthers and Speight had little hope for mercy.

It was late in the afternoon when Judge Buchanan adjourned the court and the jury climbed upstairs to deliberate. People left the saloon to mind errands, gossip, or smoke. Tess needed the break and spent a few minutes massaging the cramp out of her writing hand.

Two hours later, when the jurors clambered down the stairs, a barefoot boy sprinted through the street and yelled that court was back in session.

A somber quiet filled the packed saloon. The jury's foreman—Arnold Forrester, a local rancher—stood. The strained look in his eyes betrayed the heaviness of the duty placed on his shoulders.

"Your Honor," he said in a voice of solemn drama, "ladies and gentlemen in the court. We, the jury, find Brandon Carruthers guilty of murder. We find his accomplice, Morgan Speight, guilty of murder. We recommend that, based upon the heinousness of their crimes, both be sentenced to death."

Carruthers gritted his teeth. Speight broke down again. A chorus of whispers grew into an outburst of cheers.

Judge Buchanan smacked his gavel on the table. "Order! Order!" When the din softened to murmurs, he said, "This is no cause for celebration, only an occasion for swift application of the people's justice." He glanced at Speight, then locked eyes with Carruthers. "Brandon Carruthers and Morgan Speight," he said, in a crisp, loud voice, "this court has sentenced you to death. You will both die by hanging, tomorrow, at ten in the morning. Prosecutor, have you any final comments?"

Jackson rose. "No, Your Honor."

"Advocate for the defense?"

Hollande stood and shook his head. "None, Your Honor."

Judge Buchanan banged his gavel. "This court is dismissed. Sheriff Sanchez, you may take the prisoners away."

A wave of approving nods pulsed through the saloon, though this time no one cheered. The town of Luther had seen enough death. But justice had to be done.

Adam and a trio of deputies approached Carruthers and Speight. Carruthers spit toward Adam's boots, then sneered at the deputies as he stood. Speight braced himself against his chair, knees weak, eyes watering. Both men were led away, the chains around their ankles rattling.

Lucy and the bartender set to work rearranging the tables and chairs to serve dinner and accommodate the evening's clutch of gamblers. Tess's father left through a back door of the saloon to sit alone, smoke a cigar, drink whiskey, and contemplate life and death.

Tess, Jackson, and Hollande retired upstairs with the transcripts to complete the official record of the trial and write out copies. When she figured they were an hour from completing their work, Tess asked Lucy to ready a bath in her room. Hollande ordered supper and two bottles of wine. He didn't seem too bothered that he had lost the case. He got paid the same whether the defendants walked free, walked to prison, or walked to the gallows.

Night arrived, and they continued working by the light of oil lamps. As they reviewed the documents—the original complaint, the affidavits, the docket, the court papers—they ate chicken pot pie and sipped wine. Supper and work finished, Tess took one of the bottles to her room. A burning candle on her dresser provided illumination, and she used the candle to light a pair of oil lanterns. Wooden boards covered the bathtub in the center of the room. When she removed the boards, an inviting banner of steam beckoned her. She undressed, eased into the tub, and started on the rest of the wine. She had forgotten to bring a glass and so quaffed directly from the bottle.

Eyes closed, she let the blossoming alcoholic daze soften her recollections of the day. Her mind drifted from thought to thought like a rudderless boat. Her father would remain for the execution. That meant they wouldn't begin the return to Cheyenne until the morning of the day after tomorrow.

But those were only trifling details. The orders of the court would proceed with the certainty of the coming dawn.

And what about Adam? Tess lingered on the question. This time she wouldn't let him go. But did that mean she had to stay here? Or would he follow her? To where? Her father was ready to give up the bench and retire. Part of the reason he hadn't done so yet was to provide an income for Tess. She and her father remained hobbled together by bad luck and bad decisions.

She groped around the floor for the wine bottle, but, alas, it was empty. Disappointed and more than a bit tipsy, she let the bottle slip from her fingers and topple against the floorboards.

Assuming she and Adam did rekindle their romance, what kind of a future could she have here in Luther? As sheriff in this pimple of a town, Adam must barely make ends meet and almost certainly relied on favors to get by. Tess had long since tired of trying to live on an intermittent civil servant's salary—pin money by anyone's measure. But only Adam could assuage this ache in her heart and tend to her other desires. She daydreamed the tub had magically grown larger, and Adam—naked, of course—had slid into the water opposite her.

Adam, Burt Rex, the blacksmith, and two men deputized for the trial approached the shed beside Rex's workshop. After Speight's damning testimony, Adam knew it wouldn't be prudent to lock him up in the same cell as his gang boss. Carruthers would've strangled him. In any case, executing the condemned was the state's prerogative. Adam had Speight bound in chains and locked in the shed and posted a guard outside, while Carruthers spent his last night in the jail.

Rex keyed open the padlock, and the shed door creaked open. Speight was sitting on a pile of canvas, hands in his lap, wrists secured with iron cuffs. The chains binding his ankles were threaded through a series of iron hubs for wagon wheels. His bloodshot eyes blinked painfully at the morning light cascading in over Rex's shoulder.

"Undo his legs," Adam ordered.

Rex unlocked the chain and helped Speight to his feet. Adam and the others stepped back and guided Speight to the barn. With a nod, Rex indicated that Speight was to enter an empty stall. The outlaw understood that he was to relieve himself, which he did. Rex pointed to the horse trough, where Speight rinsed his face and cupped water to his mouth. He ran a hand over the stubble on his chin. "What about a shave?"

Adam glanced at his watch. "We don't have time. I'm sure greeting Saint Peter with whiskers on your face will be the least of your sins." He tipped his head toward a nearby table where a covered saucepan and a metal cup rested. Speight was led to the table, and he sat on an adjacent bench. Rex handed him a spoon. His hands cuffed together, Speight removed the lid from the saucepan. The escaping aroma smelled of beef stew. A hunk of bread sat on top. Rex poured hot coffee into a wooden cup, which Speight quickly emptied. Rex next half-filled the cup from a bottle of whiskey.

Speight ate slowly, relishing each swallow of his last meal. Occasionally, he wiped a tear, but he didn't break down sobbing as he'd done during the trail. Rex's children—two girls and a boy—watched from the back porch of the nearby house.

When done, Speight drained the cup of its whiskey and stood to face the deputies. They unfastened one of the handcuffs and secured his arms behind his back.

Rex led over two donkeys harnessed to a buckboard. Adam told his deputies to lift their prisoner onto the buckboard and begin the trek to the gallows.

Chapter Twenty-Two

Tess declined an invitation to ride with her father in a buggy to the execution. She joined the procession of townsfolk hiking up the main road from town, past the cemetery, left at a fork in the road and along a worn path to a grassy field. She needed the time alone and preferred the anonymity of blending in with the locals. She could've remained in the hotel. But she couldn't ignore her contributions to this fateful day, and, as an agent of the court, she might as well witness the harsh consequences of her duties.

A lone oak stood in the field. A pair of ropes twisted into nooses dangled from a thick branch, horizontal and sturdy as if nature had planned to participate in this hanging. Adam waited by the nooses, his face hidden in shadow.

Tess's mouth was dry, and her lips were chapped. She lifted the hem of her skirt to keep it from dragging through the weeds. A sudden breeze whisked over the field, rustling the oak and the surrounding trees. People assembled on the west side of the oak, men clutching their slouch hats and derbies, women their straw hats and bonnets. As they waited, they chatted quietly. Some complained about the heat and that they should've brought water.

The sounds of hoofbeats and wheels approaching brought a murmur of excitement, and people turned their faces toward the path. The crowd parted to let pass a party of mounted cavalrymen, followed by a buggy driven by Daryl Anderson with Tess's father, Mr. Jackson, Mr. Hollande, and the preacher as passengers. Last came a buckboard with Speight and Carruthers sitting in the bed, facing the rear, arms trussed behind their backs. They wobbled as their ride bounced along the uneven, rocky ground. Rex drove, and two deputies guarded them.

The buggy halted at the periphery of the oak's shadow. Except for Jackson, the men dismounted. The buckboard stopped beneath the ropes. Rex climbed slowly from his driver's seat. Once on the ground, Tess saw he limped with a cane. The other two deputies upended a bench on the rear of the buckboard. Carruthers and Speight were hoisted to their feet and then lifted onto the bench. With a six-foot drop from their boots to the ground, they were raised high enough to break their necks. Rex held the reins of the donkeys harnessed to the buckboard.

The deputies stepped onto the bench, collared the condemned men with the nooses, and cinched the ropes tight. Jackson stood in the buggy and overlooked the assembly. He pulled a watch from his vest and read the time. The men around Tess followed his example. They whispered conflicting readings.

"Nine fifty-three."

"On the nose."

"Nine fifty-eight."

Jackson withdrew a paper from inside his jacket, unfolded it, and read it aloud. It was the order condemning Carruthers and Speight to "be hanged from the neck until dead." Both of the condemned men stared into the distance, their mouths downturned, their eyes hollow with resignation. The deputies fitted black hoods over the prisoners' heads and double-checked the knots, then jumped to the ground.

Tess had the impression that the execution was proceeding with the cold efficiency of a clock. Everyone here was a gear in the mechanism, and the law was the main spring compelling them into pitiless motion.

The pastor read Scripture from the Book of Matthew and ended with a prayer and the words, "May God have mercy on your souls."

Rex nodded at Adam, who in turn nodded at Jackson, who nodded back.

Rex stood aside and snapped the reins. The two donkeys jerked forward.

The bench slid from under Carruthers and Speight and tumbled off the back end of the buckboard. The two men fell straight down and were jolted to a halt with their boots swinging three feet above the dirt. The nooses stretched their necks to obscene lengths, and, save for tiny oscillations back and forth, neither man moved.

Adam gazed across the crowd. An instant ago, their expressions ranged from disgust, to hatred, condemnation, and even anticipation. Now, as the bodies dangled from taut ropes, the collective expression was one of horror. Wide eyes blinked, faces blanched, people looked away.

He studied the two hanged men. Now at last, his secret about the stolen money was safe. He pushed aside a pang of guilt. How did hiding his part in taking some of the money and losing the rest interfere with the justice meted out to Carruthers and Speight? They'd hanged because of what they did to Nelson Cook and Francine Mills. Nothing to do with the money, or him.

Adam caught movement from the corner of one eye. To the south, on a knoll topped with buffalo grass, a man watched from atop a horse. Adam squinted at him, certain he looked familiar, but, at this distance, he couldn't be sure. He turned to

Rex, about to ask him to take a look, but, when Adam glanced back up, the man and the horse had vanished.

Tess followed the solemn parade trickling back into town. The buckboard passed them, the bodies of Carruthers and Speight laid flat on the bed.

Once in town, the people sloughed away their pensive stiffness. They became animated and even joked.

Someone had set a pig roasting on a spit in the alley between the saloon and the next set of buildings over. As Tess hadn't eaten much breakfast, only coffee and a roll, the aroma of cooked pork made her mouth water. The crowd filed into the Mountain View. Before long the saloon took on the air of a community hall, and a festive mood infected the street. At first Tess thought it perverse to indulge in such festivities after a hanging. Then she realized it was likely this town rarely celebrated anything, so to assemble as they had for the trial and the execution—and to acknowledge that law and order and civilization had prevailed—seemed an appropriate time for fellowship.

Gunter Wald offered free sarsaparilla from a large keg set on the saloon bar. Her father convened an informal court in one corner of the saloon, where he entertained a growing audience with tall tales from his past in exchange for them covering his meal, his whiskey, and cigars. It was her father's ploy to keep from having to dip into his expense accounts. Tess took a glass of sarsaparilla and chipped ice and retreated outside on a bench under the front awning. Any other time, she would've eagerly joined her father's reminiscing, but she had another priority. She waited for Adam.

The same boy who had announced the court's convening came sprinting down the street. Tess recognized him from his burr haircut and his patchwork shirt. He used a stick to guide a hoop rolling over the dirt. His scampering feet slapped puffs of dust. The hoop hit a rock and careened to the side, smacked the wall of the sheriff's office, and slid into the crawlspace underneath.

The boy skidded to a stop. Stick in hand, he dropped to all fours and peered through the planking where his hoop had disappeared. He worked a board loose and wiggled through the gap.

Tess waited for him to emerge triumphant with his hoop. Riders on horses passed down the street. She took another sip of sarsaparilla and waited. Still no boy. The crawlspace wasn't that big. Suddenly worried that something might have happened to the boy—a snakebite, a scorpion sting, or his clothes had snagged on a nail—she set the glass on the bench and walked across the street. She gathered her skirt and crouched to study the darkened crawlspace. Shards of daylight penetrated the gloom. She saw the boy squirm into the sunlight at the far side of the office. Once out, he pivoted on his knees and retrieved a bag stuffed with a small, bulky object.

The boy had found something and was keeping it a secret. Tess straightened and hustled around the side of the office. She slowed her steps as she approached the back corner. The top of the boy's head bobbed on the other side of a hay crib. She tiptoed closer.

He sat on his heels, a small cloth sack wedged between his knees. His fingers tugged at a knotted cord securing the top.

"What did you find?" she asked.

The boy jerked his head up and almost lost his balance. His face flared red with guilt. He clutched the sack. "Nothing," he replied.

"Did you find that under the sheriff's office?"

The boy didn't answer.

"Hand it over," Tess demanded. When he hesitated, she

wrenched it from him. Dirt and soot flaked off the soft cotton. Something long with square corners lay within. She set the bag on a horse rail and plucked at the knot. The boy stood and watched from the spot where she had caught him.

She kept her back to him to hide what was in the sack. The cord finally loosened, and she yanked the mouth of the sack open. Inside rested two bricks of new, crisp twenty-dollar notes.

The hair on her forearms tingled. She tipped the bricks over and saw more layered underneath. *There must be thousands of dollars here.*

"What's in the bag, ma'am?" the boy asked.

Swiftly, Tess cinched the sack and retied the cord. She looked past the boy and studied the crawlspace. How did a sack of newly minted money find its way under Adam's office?

In her mind, she reviewed the court record. The murderous affair that ended in today's hangings began with Carruthers's robbery of a courier from the First National Bank of Kansas. Two of Carruthers's men had absconded with the money and made their way to Luther, where they were murdered on Carruthers's order. Sheriff Cook then confiscated the money, which was stolen again by the gang during a raid on the town. The money was returned by Francine Mills, then stolen again, recovered by Adam, and went missing a final time when he lost the saddlebags with the cash back in the river. Since then, the money was considered lost for good.

"It's official papers," Tess said. "They probably belong to the sheriff."

"Important papers?"

"I'm sure of it."

"They worth something?"

"A reward, you mean?"

"Seems reasonable."

Tess grinned at his brashness. She hooked a finger into a

small pocket of her skirt, dug out a nickel, and gave it to him.

The boy cupped the coin and sauntered off, glancing back to Tess with a look begging to know if he'd been cheated. Cradling the bag, Tess carried it to the front of the sheriff's office. She knocked on the door, heard nothing, and tried the knob. It was unlocked.

She entered the empty office and checked the jail. Except for her, no one was present. Worried that someone might have seen this money and be tempted to seize it from her, she searched the sheriff's desk for a pistol. She found a loaded Webley in a drawer. Setting the gun within quick reach, she sat in the sheriff's chair and placed the sack on the desk.

Steps echoed on the sidewalk, approached the door. She rested her hand on the revolver, gulped once, and held her breath.

Adam pushed the door open. His eyes widened upon seeing her. When he glanced down at the sack resting on the desk, his face turned pale.

Chapter Twenty-Three

Adam stared at Tess, then at the sack on the desk. His thoughts locked up tight like wheels stuck in frozen mud. Hollow with surprise and indecision, he lost his breath, feeling so vacant that his pulse echoed through him like footfalls in an empty room. The two secrets of his life had collided, his love for Tess and the money he stole, and he feared he was about to lose both. In a bad way.

"Better close the door," Tess said.

He groped behind him and nudged it shut.

She laid a hand on the sack—the sack that contained the last of that goddamned money. She said, "I'm going to save us both the trouble of you telling me where this money came from. One, so you don't need to concoct a lie, and, two, so I don't have to listen to it."

Concoct a lie? At this instant he couldn't even say his name. The air felt liquid. He heard the creak of tack, the soft plop of hooves on the dirt street outside. Caught the light glinting off the Webley on the desk, near her hand. Tess loomed before him in microscopic detail: he could've counted the hairs on her head, the tiny bumps on her skin, her individual eyelashes, the spider web of pink blood vessels in the orbs of her eyes.

"One of the local boys found this sack under your office." She pointed to a spot on the floor where Adam had replaced the planks, the exact location where he had dumped the cash.

Slowly, breath and thought came back to Adam, and he could

speak. "Does he know what's in it?" The question came out as a feeble whisper, which embarrassed him.

She shook her head. "I took it from him before he could look inside. Though he remained strongly curious." She glanced toward the window, but it was boarded up. No one could peek in. She tapped the bag. "Haven't had a chance to count it."

"Nine thousand, eight hundred and ninety dollars," he said, cognizant of every note like they were in his hand.

She frowned. "That's an exact number. Are you sure?" She hefted the sack and, when she placed it back down, had turned its label to face Adam.

He studied the sack and froze when he realized it wasn't his. This sack was labeled *Yampa Valley Flour Mills*. His bag had only a simple stencil: *milled flour.*

Tess turned the sack over and scattered bundles of twenties. He had taken a mix of twenties, tens, and fives. This definitely wasn't his money.

Breath left him, and, as he watched her count the cash and arrange it in two neat stacks, it felt like bony fingers tightened around his throat. There was no end to the mischief caused by this infernal money.

She whispered, "Eight thousand dollars."

The number at first surprised Adam until he realized what it meant. That was the difference between what was supposedly stolen from the bank and what he'd later inventoried. He glanced at the floor, toward the hole where he'd dropped his portion of the loot. Cook must have taken eight thousand and hidden that money under the floor as well. Adam's racing heart slowed, but he remained so rigid that his shoulders and legs cramped.

Tess placed her hand on the stacks of bills. "And the number you just mentioned, that's yours?"

Adam nodded.

"Which makes a total of seventeen thousand . . ." She let her words fade.

"Eight hundred and ninety dollars," he replied.

She nodded appreciatively. "A princely sum."

"For those without money, yes."

"This eight thousand was not yours?" she asked.

"I'm guessing it was Sheriff Cook's."

"Why would you say that?"

The answer was that eight thousand had gone missing between the time Adam first counted the original bank haul and when he replaced his share with the blank paper. But he didn't say anything.

Tess grinned. "Did it come from the same source as yours?"

"You would have to ask him."

"It seems you and Cook were each working a similar swindle."

Her comment twisted into him. "It would appear so."

"And you were not in collusion?"

"I'm as surprised by the appearance of that eight thousand as you are."

"How did you plan on spending your share?" she asked. "A man in your position is suddenly flush with cash, people can get peculiar with their suppositions."

Adam's shoulders ached so much that he forced himself to relax. "I've been so preoccupied tending to the recent chaos that brought you here, I hadn't yet put my mind to the matter in question."

She pouted and shook her head. "No lies, remember? You must have thought of something."

"Very well," he allowed. "The trick is not leaving a trail that leads here. Banks record serial numbers, so, when those bills start circulating, the breadcrumbs will bring the officials straight to Luther. But if the trail starts in Mexico—"

"I'm aware of the scheme," she interrupted. "You hide your

tracks by selling the notes at a discount from face value. How much of a discount?"

Her question startled him.

"How much of a discount?" she insisted.

"Depends." While one part of his brain was trying to remember the discounts, another part of his brain wrestled with the *why* behind her question. "Fifty percent. Maybe sixty."

"What accounts for the differences?"

The *why* congealed. She wasn't going to turn him in. "I can get fifty percent in San Antonio. But the closer to the border, the higher the percentage, because there's less risk of getting caught by American banks. Provided I can avoid robbers and bandits, Mexicans will honor the notes—U.S. tender is better than their own money. By the time the bills migrate north from the border, the American banks will have no idea where they came from."

Her gaze fell on the bag. "This is a dangerous amount of money."

"I've been known to be a dangerous man." Emboldened at realizing she meant to keep this secret, he decided to reveal everything. He reached into his pocket and retrieved her letter from his wallet, then placed the soiled, tattered envelope on the edge of the desk.

Tess considered it, then pulled it close. "What's this?"

Adam kept quiet, fearful he was hoping for too much. She might yet spurn him. The irony coiled around him, that she might accede to be his accomplice but not his mate.

Her eyes lit up as she recognized her own handwriting on the envelope. She slipped the letter out and glanced briefly at what was written there. Her expression turned opaque, and Adam once more began to feel hollow.

After another minute she folded the letter, tucked it back into the envelope, and slid it across the desk. Her tight face broke into a grin. Her hand moved from the bag toward the revolver.

Adam's nerves cinched tight as new fence wire. Had he completely misread her? His mind careened with the gruesome possibility that, to save his skin, he would have to shoot her and flee like the verminous criminals he'd just hanged.

But her hand continued past the edge of the desk, toward her skirt, where it disappeared into a pocket. A moment late, her hand emerged clutching an envelope similar to his, but hers was clean, like it had been lying in a box instead of in the pocket of a wandering comanchero.

Adam recognized the letter. It was the last one he had written to her after her father told him to forget her. *Sometimes things from your past don't stay in your past.* Despite this thought, his present emptiness remained.

"I didn't keep your letter on my person, as you have mine, but I did keep it." She set her hand back on the bag of money. "In all the various ways I imagined us rekindling our relations, becoming business partners was not one of them."

The cold empty feeling disappeared, like her words were warm water poured into him. "Likewise," he said.

"And just so you don't misunderstand what our arrangement is . . ." She stood and walked around the desk. Adam studied her, uncertain of what she was up to. She approached the door and set the latch, then turned and looked at him.

He remembered that gaze, smoldering, seductive. A memory that had tormented him on many lonely nights.

The sun had set low enough for shafts of light to burn through the slim cracks around the curtain in the window. Dust motes swirled like fireflies.

Tess reached for her hair. When she pulled her hand away from the neat bun at her neck, brown curls tumbled down. Her gaze held him. His heart quickened, and his breath came in ragged gasps. She stepped in front of him and pushed him backwards, making him shuffle until he bumped into a chair and settled into it.

She lifted the hem of her skirt, revealing dark-blue, knee-high stockings held fast with light-blue ribbon. She reached for his shoulders, straddled the chair, and eased onto his lap, scooting forward until her pelvis rested on top of his.

Her hands clasped his neck, and she brought her face close. Their lips met, and the kiss was deep and glorious.

Adam ran his hands along her sides. One of her hands met his, led him under her blouse, and guided his fingers to heated, inviting flesh.

The stagecoach driver helped Tess climb the wooden steps into the stagecoach. Adam kept his distance so he wouldn't appear too familiar. She carried a small leather valise.

"Tess," Judge Buchanan said, "the interior is cramped enough. Wouldn't you prefer we stow your bag with the other luggage?"

"I prefer," Tess replied as she bent down and crammed the valise under the rear seat, "that I keep this at a convenient distance. It contains my lady's unmentionables if you must know."

The driver blushed and looked away.

Adam knew better. That valise may have contained some of Tess's unmentionables—whatever those might be—but it *definitely* held eight thousand dollars of stolen money tucked behind a false lining.

With Carruthers and Speight cold and buried, Judge Buchanan and the rest of the legal retinue—Tess, Jackson, and Hollande—were starting back to Leavenworth, Kansas. Buchanan climbed aboard, followed by Jackson and Hollande. The coach sagged and shifted with their movements as they claimed seats. Tess situated herself behind the small window at the rear of the coach. Adam watched her adjust her bonnet and pay him no mind. She played her part expertly and betrayed no hint of the romance between them.

Why did deceit always have to trail him like a shadow? No matter how straight and narrow the path he tried to walk, it always turned crooked as a snake. At last he'd been reunited with his true love, he had enough money for the two of them to live comfortably, and yet it all came bundled in lies.

The driver checked the passengers, then climbed on top of the coach and dropped into his seat beside the strongbox guard. He snapped the reins, and the team of horses lurched forward. The stagecoach rumbled away, dust lifting behind it. Adam stared at the back of Tess's head framed in the little window and secretly hoped she would turn and give him a goodbye smile. But she didn't. She couldn't.

He watched the stagecoach roll down the road and disappear from Luther.

Burt Rex stepped close to Adam. "I guess with them leaving, life here will return to normal."

"For your sake," Adam said, "I hope so."

"What do you mean?"

Adam reached inside his coat and withdrew an envelope. It contained his freshly printed calling cards. "I have business of my own out of town." Without sharing the contents of the envelope, he shoved it back into his pocket. "As deputy, you need to act in my stead while I'm gone."

Rex's hairy face sagged into a scowl. "I've had enough of playing lawman. Where are you going?"

"I have business down south," Adam said evasively. "Denver. Santa Fe. Perhaps even Mesilla."

Rex grimaced as he leaned on his cane. "When will you return?"

Adam patted his deputy's shoulder. "I'm not sure. But I'll be back. Then you can forget about being the law."

Chapter Twenty-Four

A week later, Adam entered the Planters Hotel in Leavenworth, Kansas. He removed his hat and announced himself at the front desk, and a Negro bellhop led Adam to Room 218. When the bellhop knocked on the door, Adam cleared his throat and smoothed his collar.

Quick steps inside the room approached. Adam felt his heart hitch.

"What is it?" Tess answered from the other side.

"I have a visitor for Judge Buchanan." The bellhop read Adam's calling card. "Sheriff Adam *Sancheeez* from Luther, Wyoming."

The lock clicked, and the door swung open. Tess greeted them, smiling. She wore a loose white blouse and a wide skirt. Behind her, in the suite's parlor, Judge Buchanan watched from a leather wingback chair between two end tables. His bulk filled the chair from armrest to armrest. He held a cigar in one hand that hovered over an ashtray. A corked bottle of whiskey stood on the other end table, and the judge held a short glass of it on his lap. His eyes were surrounded by deep, boozy wrinkles, the expression in them agreeable. "Why am I not surprised to see you?"

Despite her father's cheery greeting, Tess tossed an anxious glance at Adam, which only deepened the awkwardness of the moment. Adam had faced down killers, and yet the prospect of announcing his intentions for Tess to her father, *Judge Bu-*

chanan, made him tense with apprehension.

"Get in here," Buchanan demanded. "I don't think you've come all this way simply to stand in the hall."

Adam handed the bellhop a quarter and entered.

"Forgive me if I don't rise, but I've just gotten comfortable." The judge lifted his drink and continued in a gravelly voice. "Tess won't let me touch a drop until I've scribbled ten pages for my memoir." He swung the glass toward a secretary a few feet away. On its desktop rested a neat stack of papers covered in script. "Ten good pages, I must emphasize." He gestured to a trashcan half filled with discarded paper. "Fortunately, and at last, I'm finished with the first draft just as my thirst was peaking."

Adam had never known anyone who had written a book and didn't know what to say. "I'm sure it will be a fine read, Your Honor."

Buchanan sucked hard on his cigar. "Well, get on with it, and speak your mind. You didn't come here to discuss my future as a man of letters."

Adam kneaded his hat brim between his fingers. He looked down at the polished toes of his boots. Though he had rehearsed what he intended to say, the words clotted in his throat.

"I suppose I do owe you," the judge said. "Presiding over the double hanging of murderous scoundrels was a damn fine way to end a career."

"I'm obliged to have been of service," Adam managed.

Buchanan studied him. With every passing second the silence grew more oppressive. Tess remained at the edge of Adam's peripheral vision, close enough to reach in two short steps. He wanted to hug her, have her warmth reassure him, but he kept his distance. Much could go wrong if he defied society's rules.

"I may be wetter than a catfish," Buchanan sipped from his glass, "but I know what's going on. I saw it the moment you two laid eyes on each other back in Luther. What kindled between you two back East hasn't dimmed despite my protestations." His thick eyebrows cinched. "Please enlighten me otherwise if you're not here for my daughter's hand."

And our money. Adam cleared his throat. "I am, sir."

"Sheriff Adam Sanchez, you've proved yourself a capable individual, a far cry from the drifter I chased away from her in Virginia. And you're a nobler gentleman than that foppish wastrel she was unfortunately married to and had the good sense to leave behind. I've learned in my years on God's green planet that good blood lines don't necessarily make for a good man. Besides, in this arrangement, it's not my opinion that counts." Buchanan set his drink on the table, gripped the armrests of his chair, and grew red in the face as he huffed in an attempt to stand. But the effort was too much, and he relaxed. Instead, he motioned for Tess to stand closer to Adam. She grinned triumphantly.

"Very well, then," Buchanan said and reached for his glass of whiskey. "You have my blessing. If Providence couldn't keep you apart, then who am I to stand in Cupid's way?"

Adam poured himself coffee from a pot Tess kept warm on the room's heater stove. It had only been five days, but, so far, married life agreed with him. Presently, he sat at a desk table they had arranged near a window of her room.

After a civil marriage and a license that cost them seventy-five cents, Tess and Adam spent their honeymoon in her room of her father's hotel suite. They didn't have much privacy until late in the afternoon when the judge knocked himself out with his daily ration of whiskey.

Tess opened a copy of the *Midwestern States Legal Journal* on the table and jabbed a finger at an article. "California is our next stop."

Adam set his cup aside so he wouldn't spill coffee on the journal. "What do you mean?"

She tapped the page. "This relates the trial of three bank robbers and how they attempted to conceal the origins of their misbegotten proceeds through a process called money laundering."

Adam perused the article and its big words but couldn't figure out what she was getting at.

"It's what we're trying to do," she explained. "Peddle your money to hide that it's been stolen. Here, the trial mentioned that it was possible to sell heisted bills for as high as eighty percent."

The light dawned on Adam. This was the same scam he had suggested to her back at Luther. *But an eighty percent return?* "Where?"

"San Francisco."

"Then why risk crossing the border into Mexico where we could lose it all? So, I guess, California *is* our next stop."

Tess leaned across the table for a kiss. "Exactly."

From Leavenworth, Adam and Tess took the train out of Kansas and continued through Colorado, Wyoming, Utah, Nevada, and then to California. After arriving at the San Francisco train depot, they hired a cab to take them to a hotel, which was somewhat deceitfully named *The Spacious Baron,* since it was little more than a cramped, two-story boarding house. But it was close to their destination, the waterfront—the infamous Barbary Coast. As expected, the area teemed with lowlifes, thieves, and fallen women in such numbers that it rivaled both Denver and Kansas City. Adam kept his pocket revolver loaded and handy. Tess armed herself with a double-barreled derringer.

They strolled arm in arm along the boardwalk overlooking the pier. Majestic sailing ships crowded the wharf, sharing berths with steamers that fouled the air with coal smoke.

What troubled Adam was how to proceed. How could they find someone to buy their money, yet not stumble into a trap and lose everything?

As they walked, Tess kept glancing around but didn't share what she was looking for. They passed a market stall where a cluster of women—*ladies of the line*, Adam could tell—shopped for fruit and sundries. Tess slowed her steps to watch them.

"What's so interesting?" Adam asked.

"I think I can find someone who can help us." She nodded toward the prostitutes.

"How would they know anyone of use?"

"Men like to brag during pillow talk. Women are seldom impressed but remember what they hear."

Adam raised an eyebrow. "You have experience in brothels?"

Tess grinned demurely. "Court reporters learn quite a few interesting facts." She pointed to the closest saloon. "Wait there."

Well aware by now that Tess could take care of herself, Adam followed her instructions. Inside the saloon, he took a seat at a table where he could look out the open front door and ordered a beer and a plate of fried potatoes. He'd finished both, plus a second beer, by the time Tess appeared outside the door and waved. Even in the lawless Barbary Coast, respectable women weren't allowed in saloons.

Adam paid his tab and headed out to meet her. She offered her arm, and they strolled along the sidewalk.

"It cost me a gold dollar, but I found what we needed," she said. "Our man is Willard Gentry, captain of the merchantman *Sleek Wind*."

They circled toward the harbormaster's office and asked a clerk where the *Sleek Wind* was berthed. From there they proceeded to the wharf in Buena Vista Cove and found the ship tied up in its slip. It was a three-masted clipper, perhaps two hundred feet long. Empty of cargo, it rode high, and clusters of barnacles dotted its hull below the exposed waterline. The figurehead of a mermaid gazed past Adam and Tess. Chinamen hefting crates or pushing loaded dollies crisscrossed the pier, paying the two of them little heed.

Adam and Tess climbed the gangplank and stepped onto the main deck, pausing briefly to get accustomed to the gentle sway. The only worker in sight was a stevedore inspecting a stack of barrels.

Adam approached him. "We're looking for the captain."

The stevedore turned from his work and caught sight of Tess. He grinned, revealing yellowed, broken teeth. Tattoos snaked from under his ragged shirt cuffs and across the backs of his hands.

"We're here on business," she said stiffly.

"Why else would you be here?" Still grinning, he pointed aft.

Adam took her wrist, and they continued to the elevated deck at the rear of the boat. They met a tubby, whiskered man who introduced himself as Dale Johnson, the ship's purser. He led them down a short, dark corridor and knocked on the last door. Without waiting for a response, he turned the handle and cracked the door open. "Visitors, captain." The purser invited Adam and Tess to proceed inside, and he closed the door behind them.

A tall, slender man, Captain Willard Gentry was backlit by an expansive window divided into square panels. His shadow fell across the ledgers, charts, and navigation paraphernalia strewn across the table between him and his guests. Overhead, unlit gas lamps swung from hooks. The room smelled of tobacco smoke, and cigar stubs filled a ceramic cup.

As they drew closer, Gentry's face emerged from the murk. Probing eyes shone from under a thick brow, and an aquiline nose defined a long face that shaped to a strong jaw outlined by a trim beard. He wore a loose shirt, a neat tie cinching the collar. A wedding band on his left hand caught the light. Along the wall, a bridge coat and a captain's hat hung from pegs. He projected refinement and propriety . . . and then Adam remembered with humor that Tess had gotten the captain's name from a whore.

Adam made the introductions and shook the captain's large, calloused hand. Gentry offered seats, and Adam dragged two chairs close to the table. He didn't like sitting with his back to the door or that he couldn't see Gentry's hands when they disappeared beneath the table. Just in case, Adam slipped his own hand into a coat pocket and gripped the Colt Baby Dragoon.

"What is the nature of your business?" Gentry kicked back in his chair. "More to the point, why have you come to me?"

Since Tess was better with words, Adam let her speak. "We've found ourselves in a quandary, and you may be in a position to help us."

"What kind of quandary?"

"Forgive me for this act of impropriety—" Tess stood and cleared a spot on the table. She removed her jacket, then her waistcoat. Gentry frowned, looking surprised and perplexed.

Tess laid the waistcoat face down on the table. She unfolded a pocketknife and used its blade to pick at a seam. When the seam opened, she slipped her hand inside and pulled out slim stacks of bills, which she placed on the table.

Gentry steepled his fingers. "How much do you have?"

"Six thousand, five hundred dollars."

Gentry lifted a bundle of fifties and turned it toward the light. "Kansas State Bank," he muttered. He tore the band and plucked out a bill at random, then got up, collected a magnifying glass, and strode to the window, where he inspected the bill, scrutinizing it under the lens. He licked a fingertip, rubbed the bill, and looked at the paper and his finger. He pressed the bill against the window and examined it front and back, again using the magnifying glass. Finally, he returned to the table, sat, and laid the bill back on its bundle.

"Satisfied?" Tess asked.

"For now." He folded his hands and leaned forward. "I'll give you three thousand."

"Six."

Gentry at last smiled. "Four."

"Fifty-eight hundred."

"Forty-five."

"Fifty-five."

"Fifty."

"Fifty-two," Tess said. "That's eighty percent."

Gentry's smile turned neutral. "Provided I inspect more of them first."

Tess gestured to the bundles. "Be my guest, good captain."

Gentry selected bundles at random and plucked several bills from them. He scrutinized each with the same care he had shown with the first bill.

Adam listened to the ship creak around him. A rat darted along an overheard joist and disappeared into a crack in the wall panel like he'd melted through it.

Nodding in satisfaction, Gentry left the table and crouched beside a secretary desk. He opened a false door and spun the dial of a safe hidden inside. From the safe he withdrew a ledger and stacks of money that he placed on the table.

"How do you intend to spend the money?" Tess asked.

Gentry lifted his gaze, his eyes sparkling with amusement. "Does it matter? By the time your bills find their way from French Indochina to a proper American bank, a damned bloodhound couldn't tell Jesus Christ himself where they'd been."

Tess picked up each bundle that Gentry pushed toward her

and riffled the bills. Following the captain's example, she wet a fingertip and swiped it across the money. The ink didn't smear.

"We have a deal, Captain Gentry." Tess stuffed the bundles into her waistcoat, then put it and her jacket back on.

"Mr. Johnson will see you out," Gentry said, not bothering to stand. He plucked a cigar from a desk chair, struck a lucifer, and lit his smoke, puffing as he squinted in judgment at his guests. Adam didn't relax his grip on the Colt revolver until he and Tess headed away from the pier.

Close to the hotel, he relaxed enough to let go of his anxiety. Then, from the crowd across the busy street, he spied a pair of eyes locked on him and Tess. From beneath the shadow of a wide-brimmed hat, the eyes glinted like a polished blade. Adam jerked his attention to them, but they were gone in an instant. He searched for the face that framed them, but the jostling crowd had shifted, and a sea of indifferent, anonymous faces met his gaze.

"Adam?" Tess asked. "Is there a problem?"

Adam shuffled close to her. "No. I thought I recognized someone."

She gazed across the street. "Who?"

"I'm not sure." He clasped her arm. "Forget it." He kissed her cheek. "Let's make our last night in San Francisco a memorable one."

Chapter Twenty-Five

Adam peered out the window of the stagecoach as it turned straight onto the main street of Luther. The town appeared ridiculously tiny, even smaller than when he and Tess left. San Francisco had made him realize just how much of a flea speck Luther actually was. But every great city was once a hamlet, and, perhaps one day, Luther might stretch a mile in every direction.

A recent deluge had turned the street into a muddy trail. Hooves and wheels splashed through puddles. The air smelled of wet earth and sage, smoke and animal waste. Even so, it felt good to be home.

Townspeople collected on the wooden sidewalks, waving and beaming. The stagecoach, their only regular conduit to the outside world, was back again, bringing news, goods, and the sheriff and his bride. Adam smiled at familiar faces through the coach's window. Tess crowded against him and waved a gloved hand.

A paper banner hung over the entrance to the Mountain View Saloon and Hotel: *Welcome Back Newly Weds.*

Adam sighed. Ever since leaving California he'd fought the nagging fear they were being followed. Whenever the suspicion pricked him like a thorn, he'd look up, but see nothing unusual more often than not. Every so often, though, he'd catch an impression of a man looking at him. As fleeting as a ghost, this mysterious watcher, and Adam could never get a fix on who he was.

Maybe it *was* a ghost, the ghost of Nelson Cook. Such apparitions lingered after the war, when the specters of your fallen comrades took months or years to lie still and leave you alone.

Adam let himself breathe easier. He was back on familiar ground, where he was safe and surrounded by people he knew would protect him.

The coach halted close to the sidewalk. He opened the door and stood on the step, where several townsfolk greeted him with cheers. Burt Rex leaned on his cane, smiling, looking bigger, hairier, and better fed than ever, his deputy's badge shining on the lapel of his vest. Adam hopped down to the sidewalk. He stepped aside and let a ranch hand help Tess exit the coach, to another wave of cheers and applause. She took Adam's proffered arm. He touched the brim of his hat, acknowledging the well-wishers. Rex slapped his shoulder and limped beside him as they entered the saloon. The crowd followed them in.

Tess and Adam were ushered to a long table by the bar. A large cake sat there, its white frosting decorated with swirls of blue and yellow. Tess and Adam's names were carefully written on top with *Matthew 19:6* underneath.

More people slapped his back. Glasses of beer and goblets of wine were passed from hand to hand. From the kitchen, Lucy and a girl carried platters heaped with roasted chicken, pork, and vegetables, which they laid on the bar counter.

Adam let his hand slide to Tess's wrist, and they clasped fingers. He could tell she was as tired as he was, and they both would have preferred a quiet dinner alone, but they couldn't deny the town another chance for festivities, this time celebrating their nuptials instead of a double hanging.

People toasted their return. Men shook his hand. Women kissed his cheek. When the crowd subsided to enjoy the food and refreshments, Rex sidled close to Adam. "I'm glad you're back. Though it's been quiet as a deadfall on Easter morning, I'm tired of playing sheriff."

"Till tomorrow," Adam said. He tapped the blank spot on his coat where his star should've been. "Then I'll pin my badge back on."

His deputy reached into a vest pocket and pulled out a folded telegram. "This traveled on the wire as far as Rawlins, then got here via the stagecoach. This is the first ever telegram addressed to me." He treated it like a treasured memento, a symbol of his connection to the ever-changing modern world.

Adam had sent the telegram to explain his sudden and mysterious departure:

MARRIED TESS BUCHANAN STOP HAVE BUSINESS IN CALIFORNIA STOP WILL RETURN TO LUTHER FOUR WEEKS STOP REGARDS ADAM SANCHEZ STOP

Adam reached into his pocket and handed Rex a cigar, a souvenir of his travels. His deputy asked, "What are your plans now, family man?"

"No family yet," Adam replied. "Tess and I are looking to buy land just outside town. Sink a well."

"Farm?" Rex asked.

Adam chuckled. The idea of manual labor horrified him. "I'm hoping not. Tess has a little money squirreled away. Her stake in a Sacramento gold mine paid off. Enough for us to live a little more comfortably than church mice."

Rex laughed around the cigar in his mouth, and he slapped Adam once more on the shoulder before limping away.

Adam found Gunter Wald and pressed a fifty-cent piece into his hand. "Doubt you have a honeymoon suite, but give me and my missus the best you've got. We'd be pleased if you could arrange to have someone draw us a hot bath in the largest tub available."

Wald nodded, pocketed the coin, and dismissed himself.

A man strummed a bass, another beat a snare, while a woman who might have been the wife of either man played a fiddle. The trio sang and played with more enthusiasm than talent. Adam and Tess ate, drank, and danced, performing their duties as the honored guests. At one in the morning, they climbed the stairs, weary and a bit dizzy from so much alcohol. On the floor of their sitting room, their luggage waited, the light from an oil lamp shimmering on the brass hardware. A slight breeze from the open window batted the lamp's flame.

"A bit brisk for my tastes," Tess groused, as she shut the window and drew the curtains. She dragged one of her suitcases into the bedroom and closed the door.

Adam removed his coat, tossed it on an armchair, and loosened his tie. This was supposed to be their formal wedding night, but, after four weeks together, he and Tess were already well reacquainted with each other's bodies. Tonight they wanted only to ease into a tub of hot water, soak away the trail grime, and sleep on clean sheets with clean skins.

He walked toward the oil lamp to blow it out. Then he heard the voice.

"Bienvenidos." A man's voice. A whisper, gruff and threatening.

From behind a dressing screen in the corner of the room, out stepped Plutarco Gonzales—Bigotes—his Peacemaker trained on Adam. The revolver's muzzle looked huge, big enough to swallow Adam in one ferocious gulp.

Adam tore his gaze from the pistol. Bigotes glared at him, the desperado's face a wad of dark wrinkled skin surrounding menacing eyes. His stiff mustache looked as wide as the horns of a bull.

"You've been there all night?" Adam asked in Spanish. He kept his voice low as well, and calm, though his mind reeled with what Bigotes intended for him and, worse, for Tess. Could she hear them through the bedroom door? He prayed not. *Got to settle this before she walks into it.*

"I would wait forever for this moment, *desgraciado*," Bigotes answered. "And it would be well worth it."

"I admire your patience." Adam thought of his Baby Dragoon in the pocket of his coat. "And you've been on my trail, haven't you?"

"Like a shadow."

"Starting where?"

"I knew sooner or later you'd pass through Denver. Every mangy cur passing himself off as a man eventually does."

Adam ignored the insult. How to get close enough to Bigotes to wrestle the pistol from him? Adam might take a bullet, maybe two, but Tess would be warned, as well as anyone downstairs.

Bigotes glanced at Adam, then toward the armchair where the coat rested. He nodded as if to assure himself his victim was unarmed. He gestured with his gun. "Move away from the chair and keep quiet." The desperado tossed a set of handcuffs that landed between Adam's boots. "Put these on and drop to your knees." He sidestepped close to the bedroom door, smirking with anticipation. "Remember Francine Mills? We're going to relive her last night alive, when your friend Nelson Cook watched me violate her over and over again." Bigotes smiled. "Only this time, your pretty wife will be the object of my affections."

Panic and desperation squeezed Adam's heart. "The handcuffs," Bigotes ordered.

Hands sweating, Adam crouched for them.

The bedroom door opened. Tess stood in the gap, one arm holding a large towel wrapped around her body, the other arm half hidden at her side. Her bare shoulders and legs showed she was naked underneath.

Adam wanted to shout and lunge at Bigotes, buy time for Tess to escape. But it was too late; they were both trapped. Bigotes pivoted, keeping his revolver trained on Adam as he leered at Tess. "Look at her, she's as ready as a fresh *tamale*."

Adam expected Tess to recoil in shock, but she remained surreally cool and regarded the intruder as if he were a stray cat that had wandered in.

"Well, then," she replied, in Spanish. "Let's get started." She let go of the towel. It dropped, revealing her nude form. As Bigotes gaped in disbelief, Tess brought her right arm from behind her back and aimed her derringer at his head. The small pistol barked loud as a firecracker and spat fire and smoke.

Bigotes's head jerked around like he'd been slapped. His face registered shock before a veil of sadness washed over him and he turned away from her.

Tess shot him again, this time between the shoulders.

His eyes strained like he was hanging on to his last breath. Knees weakening, he leaned forward. Blood dripped from the hole in his cheek. Tess raised one leg and kicked him in the seat of his pants. He toppled toward Adam, who snatched the Peacemaker and jumped clear. As the desperado fell, Adam pumped one round into his chest, delivering another deafening gale of fire and smoke.

Bigotes landed on his side and flopped onto his back. Smoke swirled through the room. Adam's ears rang from the gunshots. Bigotes's lifeless eyes gazed upward. His mustache draped his cheeks like a black, wilted leaf. The bullet wound on his face was an ugly little hole. Rivulets of blood seeped across the rug.

Smoke curled from the twin barrels of Tess's derringer. With that gun in her hand, and her pale form blurring into the smoke, she looked like a phantasm made flesh.

As the smoke cleared and the ringing in Adam's ears faded, everything in the room seemed unreal. All he could manage to ask was, "Why did you kick him?"

"I wanted him to land on the rug," she answered as she retreated into the bedroom and slipped into a robe. "We're in the nicest room here. If he bled on the floor, we would've been assigned to another room while this place was cleaned up."

From down the hall, they heard boots pounding up the stairs.

"The way things transpired," Tess continued, "they can roll that scoundrel in the rug and drag his carcass out of here. He's bothered us enough."

Rex prodded Bigotes's corpse with his boot. Gawkers packed the sitting room doorway. Tess lingered in the bedroom, sitting on the edge of the bed, her face blank of emotion.

"My apologies for spoiling your return," Rex said.

"Why? It wasn't your doing." Adam gave the Peacemaker to Rex. "Here, you need a revolver. Take his. He's done with it."

"I sent word to the undertaker that there's a body needs tending to." Rex pointed at a couple of men in the doorway. "You and you. Roll this man in the rug and haul him out of here. Watch that you don't spill any blood, else you'll have to clean it."

Adam glanced at Tess. He wasn't sure if he felt pride or alarm that his wife had shot a man and that her biggest worry was his blood spoiling her boarding arrangements.

Chapter Twenty-Six

The hotel brought a replacement rug and a tub, which they filled with hot water. Tess insisted that Adam bathe first and quickly. When done, he stepped out and slipped into fresh drawers.

She loosened her tresses, shrugged out of her robe and draped it on a chair, then stepped into the still steaming water. She sat and bent her knees to fit into the tub. After ladling water over her shoulders, she slid beneath the surface, then sat up straight, water cascading from her face and wet hair. She looked nymph-like, unconcerned, yet Adam had not shaken off his mixed feelings about her cold-blooded reaction to killing their intruder.

"Does it bother you," he asked, "that you're right over the spot where a man just died?"

"You mean Plutarco Gonzales?" she replied. "That's so much name for an inept shootist, don't you think?"

"I called him *'Bigotes.'* 'Whiskers' suited him better."

"Regardless of his name, neither his passing nor the circumstances behind his demise bother me." She waved a hand covered in suds, then pointed two fingers to mimic the twin barrels of her derringer. "He got what he deserved. If anything, his departure from this earth was deferred too long by the Almighty's leniency."

"That's a hard thing to say." Adam dragged a stool close to the tub and sat behind Tess.

"If you didn't want us to live in a hard place, then we

wouldn't be living in Luther, Wyoming."

Adam didn't want to dwell on the topic. After so many twists and turns, their odyssey was complete. Along the way, both the good and the bad had met their ends. Like the Book of Matthew said, *For He makes His sun rise on the evil and the good, and sends rain on the just and the unjust alike.* Having seen the way the world works, Adam regarded his and Tess's possession of the stolen money as a trivial detail.

He dipped a washcloth in the water and rubbed it across Tess's back. What mattered was the future. A future with Tess, which is what he had.

ABOUT THE AUTHORS

Tomas Alamilla is a Mexican entrepreneur with a lifelong love of stories featuring Western adventure, tough cowboys, and strong women. You can find him somewhere north or south of the border.

Mario Acevedo is an award-winning editor and a bestselling author of fantasy, historical, and action novels and short stories. He lives and writes in Denver, Colorado.

The employees of Five Star Publishing hope you have enjoyed this book.

Our Five Star novels explore little-known chapters from America's history, stories told from unique perspectives that will entertain a broad range of readers.

Other Five Star books are available at your local library, bookstore, all major book distributors, and directly from Five Star/Gale.

Connect with Five Star Publishing

Visit us on Facebook:
https://www.facebook.com/FiveStarCengage

Email:
FiveStar@cengage.com

For information about titles and placing orders:
(800) 223-1244
gale.orders@cengage.com

To share your comments, write to us:
Five Star Publishing
Attn: Publisher
10 Water St., Suite 310
Waterville, ME 04901